DEVIOUS GAME

BRENTSON UNIVERSITY SERIES
BOOK 1

BRI BLACKWOOD

BRETAGEY PRESS

The subject matter is not appropriate for minors. Please note this novel contains sexual situations, violence, sensitive and offensive language, and dark themes. It also has situations that are dubious and could be triggering.

First Digital Edition: August 2022

Cover Designed by Amanda Walker PA and Design

Edited by: Ellie McLove from My Brother's Editor

Dee from Dee's Notes: Proofreading and Editing Services

Chrisandra Proofreads

EAL Editing Services

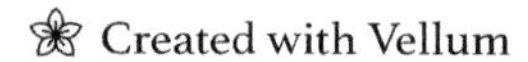

NOTE FROM THE AUTHOR

Hello!

Thank you for taking the time to read this book. Devious Game is a dark college billionaire enemies-to-lovers romance. It is not recommended for minors and contains situations that are dubious and could be triggering. The book also includes graphic violence, kidnapping, and brief mentions of a mental disorder which might also be triggering. It isn't a standalone and the book ends in a cliffhanger. The next book in the series is Devious Secret.

BLURB

I left Brentson in the dead of night and made a promise that I would never return.

I was determined to leave my past behind, but here's the thing about it:

It always has a way of hunting you down.

Now, I'm face-to-face with Nash Henson, my ex-boyfriend, heir to the Henson fortune, and crowned king of Brentson University.

He'll never forgive me for what I've done.

And when he's done playing his game with me, there won't be anything left.

Because he's determined to destroy me.

PLAYLIST

Heartbreak Anthem — Galantis, David Guetta, Little Mix
Bad Habits — Ed Sheeran
INFERNO — Sub Urban, Bella Porch
Bad Romance — Lady Gaga
EveryTime I Cry — Ava Max
Control — Halsey
Haunted — Beyonce
Break My Heart Myself (feat. Travis Barker) — Bebe Rexha
Fighter — Christina Aguilera
Out Of The Woods — Taylor Swift

The playlist can be found on Spotify.

1

RAVEN

A LITTLE MORE THAN TWO YEARS AGO

The surrounding air was electric, buzzing with excitement. Understandably so since it was graduation day. Soon-to-be graduates were sitting in white folding chairs as the ceremony progressed, while their families were attempting to document every moment.

This should have been one of the happiest days of my life, but my heart was buzzing for a different reason.

My leg bounced up and down as I took in the scene unfolding around me. Today was the day I'd been waiting for, but not for the reason most people would think. I'd been counting down to this day for years and finally it was here. In a little less than an hour, I'd be leaving this town for good.

A promise to my mother was the last thing standing between me and freedom, and I couldn't wait to exercise it. I told her I would walk across that stage, and I was determined to do it. When we were directed to stand up and walk to one end of the stage by a volunteer, I almost hopped out of my seat, too eager to get this over.

"Allison Fredericks."

I held my breath as she walked across the stage, knowing that it was almost my turn to go. After all, we practiced the day before so that we all were aware of what would be happening.

"Jamie Gibson."

I sucked in a deep breath as I was now next in line to cross the stage. I watched as Jamie shook the school principal's hand and smiled when he received his diploma.

"Raven Goodwin."

The crowd applauded, and I bit my lip as I walked up the stairs. I knew the claps were merely polite applause given at graduation ceremonies. Would it have been nice to have a host of family standing there watching me walk across this stage? Sure. But I only had one objective in mind. The lack of anyone cheering for me up there wouldn't change anything.

I heard a deeper voice cheer as the claps slightly died down. The corner of my lip twitched, but I didn't turn to face the crowd. I forced myself to continue walking forward.

"Good work." Mr. Jones, the principal of Brentson High, grinned when I reached him. I gave him a tight smile and a head nod as he held out his hand for me to shake.

Mama, I did it.

I fought to keep my feelings in check. Overcoming numerous barriers that tried to hold me back had been nothing short of a miracle. Suffering from ADHD caused its own set of challenges, but also having to deal with the only parent you've ever known tragically dying was enough to make anyone be fucked up. While some concessions had been made to help as I grieved, the wound and heartache I felt was still fresh. I took a deep breath to steady my emotions before I investigated the crowd. As I walked back toward my seat, I found a smiling face staring directly back at me.

Nash.

I knew I was going to break his heart, but I had no other choice. I needed to leave this town and fast. My plan had been to leave as soon as I got this piece of paper, but I couldn't leave without saying goodbye to him.

Even if he didn't know that this was goodbye.

I made it seem as if I, like many of the students here, would be attending Brentson University in the fall. After all, why wouldn't I want to attend one of the most prestigious colleges in the world, especially when it was in my backyard?

That wouldn't be the only dream I was giving up.

I smiled at my soon-to-be-ex-boyfriend as I walked to my seat. The connection we shared at that very moment was what I hoped I could use to concentrate on the rest of the ceremony.

My thoughts were interrupted when a large round of applause brought me back to the present. It did not surprise me that the announcer was about to say Nash's name.

"Nash Henson."

The applause only grew louder as he walked up to collect his diploma. None of this was surprising. Nash was Brentson's crowned golden boy and star quarterback. His father was the town's mayor and his mother served as one of the most involved first ladies this town has ever seen.

Which always made me wonder what Nash had seen in me. I'm sure there were "more suitable" women he could have dated, but after a teacher put us together in a group project during our junior year, we were inseparable. We made plans about what our freshmen year at Brentson would look like, even though for me, that wouldn't be the case.

Thankfully, the ceremony didn't drone on for too much longer and soon I saw my classmates gearing up to do what everyone expected of them, even when we were told not to: throw their caps in the air.

When cheers erupted around me, the bubbles in my stomach grew. The ceremony was over and it was almost time for me to leave. With former students, now alum, being allowed to move freely, it didn't take long for Nash to find me in the crowd.

Just looking at him made my body heat up, a reaction that I couldn't contribute to the heat of the sun falling on us while we stood in these long blue graduation gowns. While I felt ridiculous in this gown and had hurriedly unzipped it to show off one of the few dresses I owned, he wore it like a supermodel. From his dirty blond hair, down to his broad shoulders, and his well-defined abs. It should have been criminal to hide his physique under the button-down, slacks, and shapeless gown, but he wore it well. His tall frame forced me to look up at him if I wanted to stare into his beautiful, blue eyes.

In his eyes, I could see warmth and kindness, but most importantly, there was love. It was like a stab to the gut because of what I had to do.

"Hey."

One word was all it took to suck all the air out of my lungs. Staring back at him, a world of pain fell over me.

"Hey yourself."

"We did it."

I nodded. "That we did."

This school year hadn't been easy for either of us, but through the trials that were thrown our way, we grew stronger, and our bond blossomed. And here I was about to ruin everything.

"Your mother is proud of you."

My lip trembled and I looked down.

Don't cry, Raven.

A light breeze blew between us, and he lifted my chin up so that my gaze met his. With his other hand, he tucked a piece of my dark-brown hair behind my ear. My eyes watched his lips as he leaned forward, and they drifted closed when my lips met his. The kiss warmed my soul like nothing else. It hurt knowing this would be the last time I would see him. But it was for the best—even if he didn't know it yet.

"I love you, little bird."

Him telling me that he loved me was one thing, but him using the nickname that he'd given me was on another level. The deep breath I took was an attempt to hide the pain from my face because I knew he would be able to tell that something was wrong.

"I love you." I almost choked on the words as they left my mouth. "You should go and be with your family."

Nash looked behind him as I took a small step to the side to get a glimpse of his parents. One parent and his sister gave me a small smile while the other parent regarded me coldly. If I was being honest, that had been what I'd expected. I bit back an expression that I was sure would start something and turned my attention back to Nash. I wanted to enjoy what would be our very last moment together.

"Meet up with me tomorrow night. I would say right now, but I have family obligations that I can't get out of."

Nash's statement left no room for argument, which was why I didn't offer one. "Sure."

"I'll swing by your place at eight? Maybe we could go somewhere and..." His voice trailed off and I knew what he was getting at.

He and I had sex for the first time a few weeks ago, which was late compared to when some of our friends had done the deed. The moments we'd shared had been magical and would be something I'd always cherish. I nodded, knowing damn well I wouldn't be there when he arrived. I took a couple of deep breaths to hold back the tears that threatened to fall.

"Raven?" I turned and smiled at my best friend since practically birth, Isabelle "Izzy" Deacon. She was the only one who knew what I had planned. I gave her a quick nod and looked back at the only person I thought I would ever love. Too bad he would grow to hate me.

"I have to go."

"I should probably get going too." Nash gave me a warm smile before he kissed me once more.

After I was gone, I would always remember the feeling of his lips on mine. I said silent goodbyes with a hug that lasted way longer than it should have, and then I backed away before I could run into his arms and forget about the choice I was about to make.

I gave him a small wave before turning around and walking over to Izzy.

"You know you don't have to do this, right?"

"I have no other option."

"We can figure something—"

I shook my head. "My staying here causes a shit ton of

problems. It's best that I leave, and I'm so grateful that you're helping me pull this off."

"Of course. You know I'd do anything to help you."

I glanced at her and lost the fight with my tears. I wiped at my cheeks, not caring if I smudged the little makeup I had put on earlier today.

"Thank you. There is one favor I want to ask of you, though."

"Yes?" I saw her glance at me as I dabbed my eyes.

"Tell Nash I'm sorry. For everything."

2

RAVEN

A tear threatened to fall from one of my eyes as I surveyed the mess in the suitcase in front of me. This was it. I was really leaving this house and this town. As I zipped up another suitcase, I saw a flash of light out of the corner of my eye. When I identified that it was a car driving up to my home, my heart leapt into my throat. I wasn't expecting anyone at this time of night or at any time at all. I was too busy packing up what I could to get the hell on out of Brentson.

Could it be the police? Nothing else would surprise me at this point.

I put the suitcase next to the couch before walking over to the living room window. It wasn't until the driver of the car turned off their headlights that I was able to recognize the car and then the driver.

Why was he here?

With all thoughts of my packing left behind I dashed to my front door and stopped to run a hand through my hair and pull down the light summer dress I'd changed into after graduation. With a deep breath, I yanked the door open. I found Nash in a tuxedo standing before me.

"What are you doing here?"

"I had to see you tonight. You only graduate from high school once and there is no one else I'd rather celebrate the occasion with."

I stared at him in confusion. "But what about the family obligations? We were going to see each other tomorrow and—"

"And I didn't want to wait so I left. Temporarily. They won't miss me, but I missed you way too much."

I blushed at his words, but I doubted the validity of part of his comment. People would notice that he wasn't there because he was the Henson's only son, the golden boy of this community. Also, Nash's house wasn't far but it wasn't close either. It wouldn't take long for someone to realize that he was gone just based on how long he had to drive to get here and then back.

"But—"

When Nash's lips slammed into mine, I got the message loud and clear. More action, less talking. His hands grasped my cheeks as he brought me closer to his body. He crowded around me and everything became about getting his cock inside me as quickly as possible.

Nash backed me into the nearest wall and his hands ended up on my butt cheeks as he squeezed them before adjusting his stance so that he could lift me up.

I licked my lips as his mouth attacked my neck. The chances of me having a hickey after this were high with the way he was going at my skin and I knew that would serve as physical evidence of this moment we shared. At least temporarily it would.

When he pulled down the straps of my dress, his stare burned a hole through me. It was as if he was mesmerized by the sight of my naked breasts in front of him. He couldn't look away for fear of them disappearing. Even I recognized the irony in those words.

When he flicked his tongue over my nipple I sighed and my hand made its way into his hair. He didn't waste any time with showing my other breast attention too, but we both knew that our time together was limited. I knew that in more ways than one.

Nash took a step back and pulled a condom out of his pocket. He unzipped his pants and I bit the corner of my lip as I watched him roll the condom down his dick.

"That's awfully presumptuous of you to have a condom." My words came out rushed in anticipation of what was to happen.

The corner of Nash's lips twitched. "It's called being prepared. Now jump and wrap your legs around my waist.

I did as he said and when his cock was buried inside of me, I cried out. I cried out in pleasure because I was able to enjoy the feelings of him inside me once again. For the last time.

When he didn't move again right away, I looked at his face. His eyes were closed as if he were savoring every feeling and sensation that was running through his body. I moved against him and his eyes popped open. The heated look in his eyes was my only warning before he moved, immediately starting a pace that was almost blistering.

The only thing that could be heard between the two of us was the groans and moans that left our mouths and the sounds of our bodies connecting on a level that neither of us had ever experienced before. We'd shared many firsts together and it felt bittersweet that we were sharing our ending in this way.

"Nash," It took another moment for me to try to finish my thought. "I—I'm going to—"

My lack of ability to speak was the only encouragement he needed. His thrusts became even more powerful and there was no coming back from this. I felt the pressure in my body build and build until I crashed over the edge into what could only be described as orgasmic bliss.

My climax didn't stop Nash, however. He continued pounding into me until he too joined me on the other side. How he was still holding me up when my legs felt like jelly, especially after he too had reached his climax, I didn't know.

On top of that, he was the first to speak. "I think we got carried away."

I couldn't fight my giggles. "You think? We didn't even make it to a bed."

He examined me with his eyes before he asked, "Can you stand up?"

All I could do was nod. When he removed his cock from me, a sense of loss crowded my senses. He eased my legs down and made sure that I hadn't been lying about being able to walk. When he was satisfied that I was okay, he gave me one of his trademark smirks before he took a step back and threw the condom into a garbage bag that I'd left by the door, intending to throw out as I was walking out the door later tonight. He came back and pulled me into a warm hug.

It was a moment before he spoke. “Can I help you with cleaning up?”

Panic flew through my body. While I wanted his help in any way that he was willing to give it, I couldn’t have him walking through my house. It was a miracle that he hadn’t noticed that I’d packed most of my belongings. I chalked it up to him being focused on getting to me as quickly as possible.

“I’m good. A little sore, but okay.”

“Good. I need to get back.”

It hurt for me to watch him fix his clothes to leave, but I needed him to go. Once he was gone. I could continue with my plan and see it through.

“I love you.”

His words brought me out of the hellish thoughts I was having. “I love you, too.”

His smile widened. “I’ll see you tomorrow.”

I smiled back but waited for him to call me out on my bullshit. It felt as if I were grimacing instead. But he didn’t say anything.

Nash gave me one last kiss before he walked out of my home and I locked the door behind him. I walked back over to my living room window and crossed my hands across my chest.

Guilt filled my stomach as I watched him drive off. He didn’t know that this was goodbye and I hadn’t had the heart to tell him. That thought is what unleashed the tears that had been on the verge of falling since I’d stared at one of my suitcases before Nash arrived.

3

NASH

THE FOLLOWING EVENING

I pulled my Jaguar F-TYPE to a stop in front of Raven's house and stared up at the building. It was the first time I was taking my graduation gift for a spin and couldn't wait for Raven's face when she saw it. I knew she would shake her head in amusement because it was another lavish gift that my parents had given me. Over the top, sure, but having the hottest ride in Brentson along with the hottest girl was the perfect fit.

I couldn't wait to take Raven for a ride in it. Watching as her dark-brown-almost-black hair flew in the wind behind her, fitting her name perfectly. Her deep-blue eyes would be shining as we drove with the top down. I knew that would make her feel better, because I could see how unhappy she was at graduation.

Sitting outside of her house reminded me of how nervous she got whenever I dropped her off in front of it. She told me it was because she felt that I would judge her, but I didn't care where she lived. All I wanted was her. That nervous energy shifted once her mother had passed away, but that was understandable. Everything had changed for her, and I'd tried to be there for her as much as she would let me.

While I hadn't experienced it, I knew that losing a parent had to be awful, and I couldn't imagine that pain, especially at such a young age. Raven had shown so much grace after her mother was killed in a car accident at an intersection. She had been traveling to her second job at the time and the driver was never caught. I'd done my best to be there for her. My mother and a few others in the community had stepped up to help Raven where they could, but she'd wanted to deal with things on her own, including being forced into home ownership. Raven didn't know who or where her father was because he'd never been in her life.

My mind also drifted back to the fun we'd had the evening before. The time I'd spent with her had been way too short and I needed to get to her. I waited in my car a half a beat longer before I'd had enough. I almost threw my car door open in a rush to get to Raven quicker.

The first thing I noticed was that her car wasn't there. Had it been here last night? For a second, I hesitated, and then I remembered that she wasn't scheduled to pick up her car until tomorrow. I talked to my parents about doing more to help her because I didn't have access to more of my trust fund until I turned twenty-one. If we had to wait until then to replace her old car, then so be it. I would do my best to be there for her whenever she needed me, no matter what.

As I was walking up the pathway to her home, it occurred to me that none of the lights were on. Sure, the sun was still out, but because it was setting, it was on the cusp of being too dark to see without turning a light on.

This was strange.

I knocked on the front door and rang the doorbell but didn't get an answer. *Where the hell is she?*

Alarm bells went off in my mind. I walked around the perimeter of the home, hoping to catch a glimpse of something that would lead me to more information about where she was, but there was nothing. I pulled out my phone and called her number, but it immediately went to voice mail. The text messages we'd shared over the last day or so showed nothing out of the ordinary. What the hell was going on?

As I debated with myself about how easy it would be for me to tear down this door to get to her, a car drove up and parked behind mine. It was Izzy's vehicle.

I braced myself as Izzy exited the car alone and not with Raven. If the alarms going off in my mind weren't blaring already, this would have set them off.

"Where is she?" My voice was leveled and didn't portray any of the emotions I was feeling. Panic. Fear. Confusion.

I watched as tears welled up in Izzy's eyes before she finally spoke. "She's gone."

My heart dropped. I knew that something was wrong but hadn't been expecting that. "What do you mean, she's gone? I just saw her yesterday and we texted this afternoon. We were going to hang out tonight."

This time, Izzy let her tears fall. "I know, and I tried to convince her otherwise, but she thought this was best."

The mixture of emotions within me intensified. "Where the fuck is she?"

The tone of my voice made Izzy take a step back. I knew I shouldn't take my anger out on her, but if she knew something and was holding back...

"I don't know. She refused to tell me, knowing I would have to see you because she wanted me to give you this."

If Izzy was lying, then she was a fantastic actress because the bumbling mess she was slowly turning into was worthy of every acting award you could think of. She stretched out her arm to hand me a white envelope. I snatched it out of her hand and quickly scanned the letter, not wanting to take the time to read the letter in front of her.

"She wanted me to tell you how sorry she was."

Anger pulsed through me, clouding most of my thoughts as certain words in the letter jumped out at me. How could she do this? Our plans and dreams were intertwined with one another.

I wasn't sure what hurt more.

Thoughts of trying to track her down flooded my brain, and I even bothered to check quickly to see if she had the option to share her location on her phone turned on. Nothing. Absolutely nothing.

There was only one thing I could do that might help me find her: telling my parents about what happened. They had more money and resources than I could ever imagine, and this was the next logical step.

"I'm going to head out, but if she calls you, contact me immediately." I knew Izzy already had my phone number because of a group project we had to work on before graduation. She nodded quickly and wiped the tears that had fallen from her face. That's when something else hit me. "Are you okay to drive?"

The last thing I needed was for something to happen to her and have that on my conscience.

"Yes, I'll be fine. And I'll reach out if I hear anything."

With only a nod, I dismissed her and watched as she walked back to her car and drove away. I followed suit and walked to mine. When I opened the driver's side door, I tossed the letter into the passenger's seat as if it'd burned me. Hell, in a way, it had.

I glared at the paper resting in the seat next to me before I started my car. There would be time to deal with that later.

Although I'd pushed thoughts of what that letter contained to the side, my anger didn't subside. It only continued to brew under the surface, and I was positive I would explode later.

Questions swirled in my head as I tried to come to terms with what was going on but I couldn't wrap my brain around it.

Many had thought that there was no way we would last. After all, we were both young. My family had a lot of money and was into politics, while her mother had to work two jobs to make ends meet. Raven and her mother were fortunate that their home had been in their family for at least a generation and was paid off, while my parents owned several homes.

I'd been determined to make this work when it was clear that she wasn't. And she couldn't even tell me this to my face.

The drive to my home was silent, but my mind was a mess. My tires squealed when I slammed on the brakes in front of my house. Charles, our butler, could take it to the garage later.

I threw the car into park, slammed the car door shut, and stomped my way up the front stairs of my childhood home. I knew I must have looked childish, but I didn't give a fuck.

Raven had left without telling me to my face and my anger and hurt was the only thing I could think of.

"Good evening, sir."

"Charles." I didn't want to take the time for pleasantries.

"A letter came for you this afternoon, and I left it for you on the hall table."

I didn't verbally acknowledge what he said, but I walked to the front table and picked up the black envelope. It must have been my lucky day because it seemed as if everyone was sending me mail. I knew who sent it but hadn't expected it so soon. Now I had two envelopes, one white and one black, as if they were two pieces of a puzzle that fit together, like yin and yang. Much like my relationship with Raven had seemed to outsiders looking in. And now she'd thrown everything that we'd promised each other away.

I turned over the black envelope to open it but was stopped in my tracks by my father's voice.

"Nash."

Before I could open it, I looked over my shoulder and found my father standing in the doorway leading into the living room. He said nothing right away, instead choosing to engage me in a stare down. I narrowed my eyes in anger, not caring if he hadn't been the one to force its rise within me.

"Come with me. We have some things that we need to discuss."

4

RAVEN

PRESENT DAY

My hand tightened on the steering wheel as I drove past a familiar sign.

Welcome to Brentson

The elaborately designed sign was meant to offer a warm embrace and show Brentson's hospitality. I could see how newcomers would get warm fuzzies from it. I felt anything but welcomed.

The only thing keeping me calm was the cool breeze that felt like a gentle whisper on my face as I drove through Brentson. Late August into early September was always one of my favorite times here. With the leaves already changing, it painted a pretty picture of my hometown. What should have been a time to bask in remembering the good times I spent here was anything but. I spent many afternoons during high school at Smith's Ice Cream Parlor—still standing and as popular as ever. Many of my memories there included Nash Henson, someone I tried to forget over the years. And I failed every single time.

My original plan had been to go straight to Izzy's place,

but at the last minute, I made a detour and ended up in front of my childhood home. It had been years since I'd last been here and memories of the good times I'd had there flooded me before I could stop them. The home looked great, and I knew the team I hired to ensure my property was looked after had done a good job. That had been the only connection I'd had to Brentson after all these past two years. I'd made sure to keep the house going, and it helped provide an income for me that allowed me to move around while I went to college virtually. Thinking about my mom forced my lip to tremble, and my emotions took over and I could feel myself about to cry. I'd thought being away for so long would have mended my broken heart over having to leave my home rather quickly, but it hadn't.

I couldn't bring myself to step outside of my car, which was probably a good thing. It might also look suspicious if I was just standing in front of this home with no intention of entering. Shoving my feelings aside, I typed Izzy's address into my phone and pulled out of the parking spot in front of my house.

A few minutes later, and with a heavy sigh, I steered my old Toyota Camry onto Brentson University's campus. Another welcome sign beaconed me home and soon I was greeted by the old, yet well preserved architecture that I saw frequently as a little girl. Butterflies collided in my stomach as I took in my surroundings. What once had been my dream school was now my living nightmare. As a kid, I'd hoped I would one day enroll at Brentson. Now that I had the opportunity, it felt as if hell had swallowed me whole.

Transferring to Brentson University had been a lot simpler than I thought it would be, and for that, I was grateful. Not having to deal with that on top of everything else was crucial in helping me prepare for this move across the country.

As I continued to drive, I looked at the map on my phone before turning off the GPS. I knew where I was now. Some things had changed in the last two years, but most of what I remembered about this town had stayed the same. Recalling the last couple of directions from the GPS, I navigated to a small home and pulled into the driveway. It looked well maintained, which wasn't surprising given that it was owned by the university.

I closed my eyes and said a silent prayer of thanks. My old baby has gotten me here safe and sound. Before I had an opportunity to move, the front door swung open and out popped a petite woman with dark-brown hair that rivaled mine and a huge smile on her face.

"You're here!"

I nodded and gave her a small smile through the windshield. Seeing Izzy did nothing to calm the nerves that had taken over my body. With a shaky hand, I stepped out of the car, locked up, and took a deep breath. She bounded down the stairs and pulled me into her arms.

It felt wonderful to be reunited with Izzy. We had seen each other in person a couple of times over the years, but it had been months since we last hung out.

"Glad you made it here okay. I've been dying to hear more about why you decided to transfer here for our junior year."

There was only so much I could tell her because I needed to do my best to make sure no one else would be affected by this mess. "Izzy, I'll fill you in. I promise."

That seemed to satisfy her as a smile reappeared on her face.

"We have to get you settled. You mentioned you were having trouble finding a place, and I wanted you to know that you could always stay with me. I know there is no way in hell you'd go back home."

"I appreciate the offer, but I know I'll find something near campus."

Izzy crossed her arms in a huff. "Well, you can stay with us until you do."

I shifted my weight from one foot to the other. I knew she had roommates and wasn't thrilled about the prospect of having to stay with complete strangers, but I didn't have much of a choice right now. My move back to Brentson had been somewhat sudden and unexpected, but I knew I needed to do this. Being here right now was where I was supposed to be whether I liked it or not. "Okay."

"Yay!" Izzy exclaimed with childlike glee. "It's been way too long since we've spent time together. I've been waiting for this ever since you said you were coming back a couple of days ago." Without another word, Izzy pulled me into another hug.

"I've been looking forward to this too." That wasn't a lie. I had looked forward to spending time with Izzy. I just hadn't expected it to happen in this manner.

"Oh, no."

Izzy whispered in my ear because we were still hugging. It was clear that something was wrong. When her arms loosened and I regained the ability to move, I looked over my shoulder before doing a one-eighty. Standing across the street was the last person I was ready to see again.

My breath caught in my chest when his eyes landed on me.

Nash.

He still looked as handsome as I remembered. His dirty blond hair was shorter than it had been in high school and while he was fit in high school, he'd filled out even more and bulked up in the years since I'd seen him last.

Any hope I had that he might have forgotten all the things I did was dashed when his eyes narrowed. He glared at me. Based on the look on his face, I knew if he could have snarled at me from where he was, he would have. Or so I thought. After all, I didn't know him anymore.

Nash wasn't alone and soon the guy that I didn't recognize drew his attention away from me. But, as he left, he gave me one final glare.

I watched him walk away, not blaming him one bit for his reaction. Hell, based on what I did years ago, I expected it to be worse.

My name might be Raven Goodwin, but I was far from good.

5

NASH

I knew my eyes were playing tricks on me. There was no way in hell that Raven Goodwin dared to show her face back in Brentson. After what she did, she couldn't think that everything would have been gone and buried. It had been twenty minutes since I'd seen her and yet the image of her burned in my memory.

That lying bi—

"Nash, dude! What the fuck?"

Easton's question made me look down at my hand and found that the coffee I'd ordered ten minutes ago was now all over my hand because of me crushing the cup. Easton stared at me before throwing a shit ton of napkins my way. "You better clean every drop of that up too."

"Or what?"

My question wasn't much of one. It was my daring him to list the consequences that both of us knew would never come to fruition. After all, he knew where he stood and that I wouldn't take any shit from him. The glare he sent my way told me he wanted to say some slick shit, but he didn't. Good. It was the smartest thing he'd done all day.

"Nash, can I help you clean this up?"

I smirked at Easton before turning to the girl that randomly appeared. "Sure."

I cleaned my hand while she cleared the liquid on the table. Easton shook his head as we watched the scene unfold in front of us. Another girl walked over, and I recognized her as the one who'd served us our coffee when we arrived. I gave her a small smile as she handed me a fresh cup and watched a blush creep up her face. Easton also noticed it and rolled his eyes but said nothing. He waited until we walked out of the eatery before he spoke a word.

"You know, you are the luckiest son of a bitch I've ever met."

I shrugged. This behavior wasn't out of the norm for me, and for as long as we've known each other that had been the case. In fact, he'd benefited from it on more than one occasion.

We walked out of the eatery, allowing the stares to follow us as we left. It was something that usually happened, and I'd grown used to it. Being the son of the town's mayor and quarterback of the Brentson University Bears had a lot of advantages, including getting local and national attention.

"Listen, man—"

My ringtone cut Easton off. I pulled out my phone and saw that it was my father.

"One second," I said before answering. "Yes?"

"I wanted to remind you about the dinner you're coming to tonight."

"I didn't forget." And I hadn't, because how could I? He or

my mother had been reminding me about it every other day for the last two weeks. Also, this would have been fine as a text message instead of a phone call.

"Be twenty minutes early so that there's no chance you'll be late."

I looked to the sky before I glanced at Easton. Between running into the girl who attempted to ruin mine and my family's lives and this shit, I was bound to lose it. "I'll be there."

"Thanks. See you in a few hours."

He hung up before I could, and I put the phone back in my pocket.

"Let me guess." He paused while he pretended to think. "Your dad."

"What gave it away?"

"The look of annoyance on your face?"

That was a fact and was growing more and more apparent each day. When your father was the current mayor of a town, it was instilled in you to keep up appearances and if you did anything that could become a headline, to either keep it under wraps or have it buried. I wouldn't deny that I had done plenty of shit that should have made front-page news in Brentson but didn't because of my parents' tenacity to succeed no matter what.

With the support of my mother, my father's next goal was to run for the governorship of New York. Although he was remaining coy in public, the decision was final. It was one reason they requested that I attend a small dinner party at their home tonight. If I had made plans tonight, it wouldn't have mattered. My father probably would have just asked my mother to call me to turn on the waterworks in order to guilt trip me into attending. Same shit, different day.

This isn't to say that I don't like my parents. It was just that sometimes their focus on my father's political career trumped things that were important to me.

After saying goodbye to Easton, I walked through the lobby of my apartment building and greeted Oscar with a tight smile. When I walked off the elevator and reached my front door, I slammed the door shut. Having this entire place to myself and not having to deal with other people, especially since I was in a foul mood, was fantastic. While it might be extremely extravagant for a college student, I didn't give a fuck.

Sure, the doorman was overkill and some of the amenities were too much, but we had to keep up appearances as much as possible. We could afford it and Mayor Henson refused to have his only son living in a slum.

My mother and an interior designer had taken the time to create the look and feel of this apartment because I didn't care. I had a place to do what I needed to do to get ready for the day and to sleep at night. All of the extra fluff was nice, but with everything I had going on with my schedule, at times I was hardly here. I did have to admit that the white, grays, and browns that were prevalent throughout the space were what I liked, so they'd done a great job there. Dad didn't care about the design either, but it did make a nice backdrop for a profile a reporter did on our family a few months back.

Sometimes, just the thought of my father would enrage me. However, annoyance with my father slowly morphed into irritation with myself because even now I couldn't get Raven out of my mind.

What the hell was she doing here?

The anger I felt toward her resurfaced immediately when I saw her face. It would be a lie for me to say I hadn't thought about her over the years. We'd been high school sweethearts who had promised to conquer the world together until she threw it all away.

And then I found out from my father why she'd left.

I rolled my eyes at myself for spending another second thinking about her. I strolled over to my closet and found a custom-made black suit, white dress shirt, black tie, and black shoes. If I looked like I was going to a funeral, so be it. It felt as if I was.

Since I still had a couple of hours to burn, I went to grab a beer from the fridge. My progress was halted because the doorbell rang. Usually if I had any visitors, my apartment's doorman would call up to my place to ask if I was expecting anyone or wanted them to come up and see me. Seeing as how none of this happened, it must be something else.

I glanced through the peephole before opening the door. It was Oscar with a huge smile on his face. It had to be fake, because who the hell would be this cheery every second of every day?

"Mr. Henson?"

"Yes?" I was used to being referred to as so.

"This came for you. They asked me to deliver it immediately."

Who was they? I looked down and saw that he was holding a black envelope and everything clicked into place. Only certain people knew everything that this envelope contained, and now it was my turn to find out. I did, however, have a good idea of what was in it. It was something that I had been preparing for during most of my college career.

I didn't take the envelope right away and I could see Oscar staring at me with curiosity beaming in his eyes. That curiosity would have to remain because there was no chance in hell that he would know what lay on those pages.

"Was this it?" I asked.

When Oscar confirmed that it was, I took the black envelope out of his hand and whispered my thanks before closing the door behind me.

Without opening it, I knew what at least part of the letter would say. In a few days' time, it would be time for the Chevalier Leadership Trials to begin.

I had some time to burn before I needed to get ready, so I tore open the envelope and read its contents:

Dear Nash,

You've been selected to be one of the representatives of the Eagles as we start the process in selecting our next leader. You are to appear at Chevalier Manor next Sunday evening at 9 p.m. where you will await your first task. More information will be provided when you arrive.

Sincerely,

Tomas

Chairman of the Chevaliers, Brentson University

I leaned back against my countertop and let the words run through my mind repeatedly. It was something I'd been waiting my whole collegiate career for and now it was here.

I'd shown my dedication to the Chevalier's mission, and it had paid off. I was forging my own path and I was now one step closer to achieving my goal of becoming the next chairman of the Brentson University chapter of the Chevaliers.

IF I HAD to give someone else another tight smile, I was going to lose my shit. I didn't want to be here, and I would have thought that my annoyance was apparent. It didn't seem to matter because several of my parents' guests had no problem coming up to me to shake my hand and engage in small talk.

Many of these people were in the room to kiss my ass. I was used to it, but my patience for it tonight was nonexistent. I didn't want to socialize, and I'd much rather be at home cracking open a beer than dealing with this shit. I knew many of the people that were here were hoping to get hired by my father as he explored the possibility of running for higher office. This was an opportunity for my dad to smooth talk them, gain intel, and make a decision on whether he would want any of the people in this room on his team if he decided to run. I almost snorted because there was no chance in hell that he was not running.

Suddenly, I was elbowed in the gut, I looked down at the place I was hit before looking up at the perpetrator: my little sister.

She leaned over and said, "Could you at least look like you want to be here?"

"Could you at least pretend that you're not drinking while underage?" I gestured to the glass of wine in her hand.

Bianca shrugged and took an exaggerated sip from her glass before she cut her eyes over to me. "It's the only way to make this evening more bearable."

She had that right. "Dad's going to come over and be pissed about... this display because you're still underage"

"Let him."

I couldn't help but smirk because she'd learned from the best. I enjoyed that she didn't let our parents' ambition affect whatever she was going to do. It was one of the many ways we'd gotten our payback on them when we were the furthest thought from their minds while they decided to make decisions that would affect us.

I had to admit it was more my father than my mother, but she tended to go along with what he dictated. She didn't see a reason not to, because in her eyes, he was never wrong.

Until he did the unthinkable.

The clinking of a spoon on a glass brought our attention to the front of the room. There stood my parents in all their glory.

Van Henson stood tall at the front of the room with a navy suit on that cost more than some people made in a year. My mother, Elizabeth, matched my father's suit with a white dress, and together they made a stunning couple. Picture perfect was the best word I could have used to describe them together. While they both had their demons, they sure knew how to keep up appearances when the time came.

My mother gestured for Bianca and me to come toward them, and I stepped to the side so that my sister could walk in front of me. My father us both small smiles as we took our place next to them before addressing the crowd.

"Welcome to our home. If you need another drink before

we head into the dining room, please don't hesitate. Once we sit down at the dining room table, dinner will be served momentarily, and then we can discuss what lies ahead."

After Dad was done talking, our family turned around and walked toward the dining room. When we were several feet ahead of everyone else, my father leaned toward me and said, "Good job, tonight. Keep it up."

His words were supposed to be encouraging, but there was a hint of something else lying underneath. There was disappointment and him daring me to fuck up this night for him, but that wasn't the only thing. Something he would never outwardly admit to, but I knew better.

He didn't want to piss me off because he didn't want to ruin any chance of me achieving what he hadn't been able to: Chairman of the Chevaliers.

6

RAVEN

The wind had picked up today, but that wasn't the reason I'd shivered. It was because the stares that followed me as I walked into Virgil Cross Center were unsettling. Some people averted their eyes once I got closer to them, but others stared as if they were watching a car crash happen in front of their very eyes. Hell, maybe they were.

"Ignore them, Raven. Soon your return will be old news," Izzy whispered to me as I readjusted my backpack and continued on my way.

Having lived the last two years away from here and being kept in the shadows for so long hadn't prepared me for being the center of attention. I thought that since we were all now in college, no one would give a shit about someone new transferring in, but clearly, I was wrong. Some people I recognized from high school at Brentson High, but there were a few unfamiliar faces.

I didn't focus on that thought too much on the drive back to town, but it's clear I should have. Maybe I would have been better prepared then, but I expected that we all would have moved past the high school mentality that was on display right now.

I was clearly mistaken.

Keep your eyes on the prize, Raven.

I thought back to the letter that was now buried in one of my suitcases, an attempt to hide its contents from the world. Instead of hiding my face because of all the stares that I was getting, I walked in with my head held high, eyes focused ahead. The letter was almost ingrained in my brain by now.

If you want to know what happened to your mother, you will come back to Brentson. You will receive further instructions soon.

I remembered that line like I'd just read the letter. The very next day, I received a packet in the mail, welcoming me to the Brentson University family. I knew that must have been the further instructions the letter was talking about. Strange? Yes, but I would do anything to learn more about the day that my mother was killed. If this brought me the closure that I'd never received, then I was willing to take it.

The whole thing was creepy. How this letter had found me when I hadn't told anyone where I was outside of the property manager that I hired. How they'd managed to get me enrolled into Brentson University, a prestigious institution, without my knowledge. These are the things I hadn't told Izzy because I was afraid that I would sound like I was losing my mind.

I pushed the memory down and leaned forward toward Izzy. "No one has forgotten what happened when I left," I whispered to her.

"I mean, it was a big deal for this town. Plus, no one got to hear your side of the story."

She was right, and I could hear the underlying meaning of what she'd just said. Izzy also didn't know the full scope of why I'd left Brentson, and I'd done that on purpose. I didn't want another life to be ruined because of me.

After I'd left town, I looked up our local newspaper while I'd been on the road and stories about what I'd done had been reported for months. It was clear that the paper had been grasping at straws when it came to 'cracking the Goodwin case' and figuring out why I'd skipped town months after my mother's death. While some assumptions had been interesting, none of the solutions that had been said were correct. No one would ever know what went down unless the people involved gave a breakdown of what happened. And it sure as hell wasn't coming from me. I'd already lost enough and didn't want to lose any more, if I could avoid it.

I could lie to myself and tell myself that none of it mattered, outside of what I needed to do, but it did. All of this mattered, but I refused to let their stares and murmurs distract me from what I had to do.

Don't let them catch you slipping.

I let my mother's words flow over me as I pushed my shoulders back and stood up straighter. I wouldn't shrink under their gazes.

Things got better once we were making our way through the dining hall and could finally sit down for lunch. The attention shifted from me to the daytime television shows that were on and seemed to enthrall the masses here. Not that I blamed them.

The only thing that could have made this worse was seeing Nash. Thankfully, that hadn't happened, but the way my day was going, I wouldn't be surprised if I ran into him. The nervousness I felt at the prospect of running into him reminded me of when he first noticed me during Mrs. Lehman's history class in our junior year. I knew he was out of my league when we first met, but he was determined that we would be together and that he would prove to me that he was right. And he did until I took off out of Brentson like a bat out of hell. Hell might have been a nicer place than Brentson would have been if I'd stayed.

"That was interesting, to say the least." Izzy's comment interrupted my observations.

"Tell me about it," I said as I bit into the small slice of pizza I'd grabbed from one of the food stations.

"It could have been worse, right?"

"Given my history? Yep."

That led Izzy to snort, and I fought back a grin. It diffused some of the tension that had grown because of my entrance into the dining hall.

"How did your classes go today?"

I welcomed Izzy's changing of the subject because this should have been the biggest thing I had to deal with today. While it still was, the stare down I had just endured almost took its thunder.

"It went well. I'm glad we left your apartment earlier than planned because I got lost on the way to class."

"My directions didn't help you?"

Izzy had walked with me part of the way to the building where my first class was held, but once she left, it didn't take much for me to get lost.

"It did, but I made a left instead of a right, and then got all turned around because of it."

"Oh, I'm sorry," she said.

"It's not your fault. You tried your best, and I think between not being familiar with the campus yet and being nervous about my first day, I set myself up for a disaster. I found the library, though."

Izzy made a face. "Not going to lie. I try to avoid the library as much as possible."

"Of course you would. There isn't much partying going on there, so why would you go?"

"Ouch. I'll let that burn go because I'm trying to be a better person."

There was no way that she could say I was wrong, however. While Izzy did well in school, according to her, she had been doing her best to party hard since she was almost twenty-one. I couldn't blame her, even though it wasn't my vibe.

"In order to make it up to me, I'm dragging you to one of Brentson's parties, whether you like it or not."

"Do I have a say in this?"

"Nope, not one. And that's in addition to my twenty-first birthday party."

I raised an eyebrow at her. "Why does this sound more like an excursion than just a house party on campus?"

Her grin grew and almost took over her face. "Because it is. Once I've finalized details, I'll let you know."

I shrugged. "Fine. Whatever."

"Great!" Izzy said overly enthusiastically. She studied my face before her mood mellowed. "If you don't want to come—"

"It's fine. I swear."

Izzy eyed me before taking a sip of the iced coffee she'd

ordered. I could feel her judgment from here. Her dark-brown eyes focused on my blue ones.

"I'll be there. At least for your twenty-first. I've missed several birthdays and I want to be here for this one." That went both ways because I celebrated my twenty-first by myself about a week before I drove to Brentson.

Izzy gave me a small smile, confirming my statement. While I'd sent a quick text acknowledging it, it wasn't the same as being there to celebrate with her in person.

She leaned in closer to me and whispered, "I never held any of this against you. I understood why you left, and I don't blame you at all."

Her vote of reassurance swept over me and made me feel at ease but only for a moment. She didn't know half of what had gone down with me, and I wondered if she would feel the same if she'd had the complete picture.

"Thank you." It was the only thing I could think of to say.

Izzy waved me off. "Don't need to thank me. I have your back and defended you when the news broke."

If I wanted to be honest with myself, I wished she hadn't publicly supported me all those years ago. Thankfully, she received little backlash due to taking a stand in my favor. From what she'd said after I'd been gone for a few months, things had slightly quieted down as the years had passed and while what occurred was brought up, it had become almost like an urban legend. Until now.

Would it be beneficial to clear my name? Potentially, but I also worried that the risk of doing so would be too great. Everyone had already formed an opinion of me in their minds, so what was the point?

Never mind the fact that the summons I'd received made

that significantly more difficult. Instead of choosing to continue to make conversation with Izzy, my eyes landed on the plate of food in front of me as suddenly my appetite vanished after I'd thought about the letter I'd received.

I sighed and continued to push around the food on my plate as the feeling of dread crept back into my mind. When I glanced up from staring at the food in front of me, my eyes connected with several other students who turned to look in my direction. When our eyes met, they shifted their gazes back to mind their own business instead of mine. Without a doubt, I knew this was going to be an interesting year at Brentson University.

7

RAVEN

I groaned as I looked at the book that was open in front of me. This paper wasn't going to write itself, but I couldn't convince my mind of that. Instead, I leaned back in my chair and rubbed my hands over my face. This assignment could wait for a few more minutes.

I leaned back in my chair with my eyes closed, allowing the music coming through my earbuds to take over the thoughts roaming my head. I needed the distraction but told myself that it would be temporary. Maybe a visit to Smith's Ice Cream Parlor would be a justifiable reward for being here, even if I hadn't gotten all the things completed that I wanted to get done.

The library had become my home away from home. It's where I was beginning to feel most comfortable. Izzy's apartment was pleasant, but she had three other roommates. While they weren't rude, they weren't exactly welcoming either. Part of me understood that, given my arrival was quite sudden. All of this meant I needed to find a place to stay out of everyone's way, and for me, that was the library.

I'd chosen a quiet corner on the second floor and was busy highlighting passages from one of my history textbooks. Or at least trying to.

My brain refused to focus on the words on the page, no matter how hard I tried. This wasn't unusual for me, but normally my ADHD medication would see me through. Today had been one of those days where I hadn't taken my meds, and now, I was paying the price. The dull headache that was forming near my temple wasn't helping matters either. It wasn't that what I was reading was boring. History had been something I was interested in, so it wasn't that.

Instead of trying to force it, I took out the ponytail I'd thrown my hair up in when I arrived and closed my eyes and tried to soothe any pain before it got worse. Placing two fingers on the side of my head and rubbing in circular motions helped, but maybe it was a sign that I needed to head back to the apartment.

When I opened my eyes, my hands shot to my mouth to prevent any sound from escaping. Of course, Nash Henson would choose to be on the same floor as me at the same time as me. What were the fucking odds?

There was no way I could duck out of the way without him potentially seeing me. I put my head down as if I was reading the words on the page in front of me and hoped like hell that my hair would be enough to cover my face. He was talking to another guy quietly, so I hoped it was enough to distract him. I held my breath as I waited for him to pass by.

When he didn't approach me, I let out the breath I'd been holding. I didn't see which way he'd gone, but I considered this a win.

After seeing him, I knew there was no way I was going to

get anything else done. Then again, it wasn't like I was getting anything done before he showed up. I packed my bag, tossed one strap over my shoulder, and walked away from the table I'd been stationed at for the last couple of hours.

As I was cutting through a row of bookcases, a hand latched on to my upper arm and before I could scream, a hand slammed down over my mouth. I could feel myself being dragged backward as I struggled against my assailant, but it was no use. The person was bigger and stronger than I was. I looked around while trying to grab at the person's hand, hoping that someone would see what was going on or that there were cameras nearby, but I saw no one.

There was a slight pause in our movements as I heard a door unlock behind me and I hoped this might be a chance for me to get away, but it was no use. It was then I realized that I'd been dragged into what looked like a hallway. It wasn't until the person had thrown my back up against a hard surface that I realized I was in a stairwell and that my attacker was Nash.

"Ow!" I cried out, but my words were muffled because his hand was covering my mouth.

Nash leaned down to look me straight in my eyes. Fear grew within me as I wondered what he was going to do next. "I'm only going to tell you this once. No one wants you here, Goodwin. Fucking leave and go back to whatever shit hole you climbed out of. After all, you're good at that."

The disgust on his face made it evident that he was talking about himself and no one else. The way his aversion to me dripped off his tongue as he said my last name made me feel disgusting. His words slid across my body, leaving a thousand stab wounds in their wake. When we were dating, he'd never referred to me by my last name. As much as I hated to admit it, this hurt on another level. I didn't realize he would still have this effect on me. I thought that with time, both he and I would have moved on, but by the standoff occurring in front of me, time hadn't healed all wounds.

When my words came out garbled against his hand, he said, "I'm going to remove my hand, but if you scream, yell, or make a sound that could alert anyone to where we are, you're going to regret it. Understood?"

I nodded my head. When he removed his hand, I was temporarily stunned by what had just occurred and the slight pain in my back from being thrown against the wall. Without a doubt, I knew he could have thrown me against the wall harder, and I wondered why he hadn't done so. Was this only a warning of what was to come?

Wetness formed in the corner of my eye, and I prayed it wouldn't fall or result in more tears. While I wanted to wince and shrink up into a ball, I kept a straight face, refusing to give him the satisfaction that he'd just both physically and mentally hurt me.

"Now repeat what you said."

Before I spoke, I took a deep breath. "I said, you're only speaking for yourself so you can take your opinion and shove it. I don't care what you think anymore, and I haven't for a long time."

For a brief second, he seemed surprised by my response. His shock didn't last long because then he said, "You've become a bitch since you've been gone."

He said it so matter-of-factly that I almost laughed. I was surprised by my reaction. Him calling me a bitch would have normally set me off, but here I was calm as could be. Outside of the name calling, his reply was valid. When I was in Brentson last, I did my best to shrink myself. Not making waves was how I survived high school, but this wasn't high school anymore. Since I'd left, I'd changed.

That shouldn't have been surprising, though. Although it had only been two years, they'd been the hardest years of my life. It had been important to me to become an advocate for myself because the only one I have been able to count on was me.

Before I could say anything else, Nash spoke again.

"Watch how you speak to me." His voice deepened. The only other time I'd heard Nash's voice become that deep was when we were making out and he wanted to take things further. This time, however, it was laced with a warning that I was treading on thin ice with him. But I didn't care.

All signs were cautioning me to back off and to walk away while I still could, but I refused to convince myself to do so.

I stood up, determined to show that he wasn't going to bully me into silence. I was here to find out what happened to my mother, and I wasn't about to let this asshole do anything to prevent that from happening. As my eyes traced his body, it was then I remembered just how much taller he was than me. His body used to bring me so much comfort, but now it intimidated me.

I steeled my spine before I asked, "Who the hell made you dictator of Brentson?"

The fire burning in his eyes increased in intensity. I remembered the things that would piss him off, the things that would make him tick, but I wasn't used to being on the other side of his rage. And it was obvious that he'd changed over the years too.

At least his feelings for me had. Not that any of this was shocking given what I'd done. A tiny bit of regret about me leaving Brentson the way I had entered my heart even with his blue eyes boring into me, daring me to say something else he didn't like.

I swallowed hard and shifted my approach when it came to this conversation. "Look, Brentson is a huge campus. We can coexist here and when we run into each other, we can just walk on by."

He scoffed, leaning closer to me once more. "You make it sound so easy."

I refused to hold back my words. "That's because it is. We are both adults here and can stay as far away from each other as humanly possible."

I glanced at the door that Nash had dragged me through, hoping that someone would walk through and put an end to this discussion. "It would be much easier to do that if you went back to wherever you came from."

"That I can't do, Nash. I'm here now and you'll just have to deal with it. I promise I won't bother you if you don't bother me."

Saying his name to him again felt weird. For years, I'd thought about him by only saying his name in my head, but now I was here, standing in front of him.

"That won't work for me."

"Oh? And why is that?" I crossed my arms over my chest and watched as Nash's gaze drifted there. He didn't try to hide the fact that he was staring at my breasts one bit. I rolled my eyes and cleared my throat, dragging his attention back up to my eyes.

"Because my hate for you is alive and well. I'm going to make your life a living hell."

As I stared into his eyes, the ones I once thought held my future in them, there was something that hadn't changed. I knew he was dead serious and that without a doubt, he meant every word.

8

NASH

I'd tried to talk myself out of coming here at least fifty times, but I still turned my car onto this street. I parked my sedan across the street from Raven's apartment and turned off the engine and my headlights. My slightly lowered window allowed me to hear some of the sounds around me. It had been a good idea to not drive my sports car today because it would have drawn more attention to me. Though I could feel the tension rippling off of me in waves, a small part of me enjoyed sitting in the darkness and the peaceful nature of it all.

Except there was nothing peaceful about the woman that lived in the house across the street.

What I couldn't explain to myself is why I'd chosen to drive here. It was out of the way for me to come here, yet here I was. Something was drawing me to be here, and I didn't know what. Sitting outside of her home wasn't a part of my plan for the rest of my evening, but here I was. And that still didn't force me to put my car in drive and tear out of this parking space.

I was able to confirm that she was still here, even after my warning at the library several hours ago. The beat-up car she'd walked out to when I'd first seen her was parked in the driveway. I had my answer about whether she'd left town or not and still I sat here. Seeing her still here was irritating as fuck, but I did think she was tenacious.

Too bad this same energy was nowhere to be found when she vanished right after we graduated. If she would have come to me, trusted me instead of betraying me, maybe things would have been different. The hatred, anger, and rage that I feel toward her wouldn't exist.

I'd known she was studying in the library before she sat down. I had eyes all around this campus, and if I wanted to know something, I didn't have to lift a finger to find out.

Well, there was one thing I didn't know, and only one person could tell me.

Why the hell did you come back, Raven?

But I couldn't go up to her front door and demand that she speak to me. At least not yet. Instead, I was gripping my steering wheel as I looked up at a window near the front of the house, wondering if that was the room she was staying in. What the fuck was happening to me?

Ever since she'd arrived back in town, my brain has been a fucked-up mess. It didn't matter that my surprise at seeing her for the first time in what felt like forever had caused a dozen different emotions to filter through my mind at a hundred miles per hour when I'd first laid eyes on her.

I couldn't afford this distraction right now and that was one reason I wanted her to go back to wherever she'd been for the last few years. Things had been good and the hurt and betrayal that I felt after learning she was gone had faded. Or so I thought.

Everything in me was telling me to drive away, but I was cemented in this spot. There was nothing to see here, and I had to figure out another way to get her out of here, and it might require more drastic measures. That would have to wait until after tomorrow.

When my phone vibrated beside me, I jumped slightly because I hadn't been expecting it to make a sound. I looked at my dashboard and pressed the button on the screen to open the text.

Unknown Number: ***What you're doing could be classified as stalking, N.***

I didn't recognize the number, but the area code was from Brentson. If whoever was doing this was trying to frighten me, they had another thing coming. Instead, it pissed me off because how dare someone watch me... while I'm sitting here.

The irony wasn't lost on me. I looked around to see if I could see anyone, but there was no one to be found. There had to be some way that someone was tracking me, but who? And how?

Out of the corner of my eye, I saw a flash of light before I heard an engine start. A dark-colored SUV I hadn't noticed before turned its headlights on. I hadn't noticed anyone drive down this street or enter any of the other parked cars that were currently idling on this block. So, who the hell was that? And was that the person who had just sent me the text message?

Why was I wondering about a random car on the street? It was because Raven's arrival has really screwed me up. All of my thoughts were centered around her, but I couldn't let this continue.

The Chevalier trials were beginning tomorrow evening, and I needed to be focused on that. I also needed to pay attention to football, because my next game was only days away. Balancing practice, training, and meetings with the Chevaliers had taken up most of my time. Now there was this.

While the SUV was pulling out of its parking spot, I spared one last glance at the window. Nothing had changed since I'd arrived, and I was finally able to convince myself to leave. I waited until that dark SUV pulled off and drove down the street before following its path into the night.

The driver didn't do anything out of the ordinary and as I was reaching the city limits, I was forced to stop at a stoplight while the SUV in front of me was able to squeak through. I rolled my eyes because I was frustrated, and then it hit me: why had I gone after the SUV anyway? Yes, there was curiosity, but I knew it was more than that. I'd had plenty of other things I needed to do, yet I'd followed an SUV that had made me suspicious outside of my ex-girlfriend's house.

If anyone could see me now, they would wonder if something was wrong with me. That wasn't enough to convince me to stop attempting to follow the vehicle. I drove about half a mile more before I decided that there was no way I was going to catch up with that SUV and I turned around. For the rest of the ride, I berated myself for going out of my way to begin with, and then for it ending in a wild goose chase.

9

RAVEN

I stumbled out of the bedroom I'd been staying in and into the main living area of the apartment. I'd been very fortunate that one of Izzy's roommates had to pull out for the semester at the last minute and I was able to take her place. Our landlord had no issue with it and Izzy loved it. Her—and now my—roommates seemed to tolerate it because at least they weren't having to fork over more money for the rent.

The apartment was light and bright, and I assumed that they'd decided on the color theme because it was a neutral option that would blend well between everyone's styles. It would also make it easy when we all moved out and we wouldn't have to do any painting. Hopefully.

I pulled the brown chair away from the dining room table and threw myself into the seat. My head landed on my arms, cushioning it from hitting the table with a loud thud.

It was too early in the morning for me to be up, especially when I spent most of the night tossing and turning in my bed. My encounter with Nash yesterday still ran through my mind on repeat. No matter what I tried to do, I couldn't shake the feeling that came over me when I thought about Nash shoving me up against the wall. I don't know what I'd expected if I had to see him again, but it hadn't been for him to find me in the library and threaten me.

Part of me wanted to tell someone, the authorities or Izzy, what had happened to me. Deep down, I knew telling anyone with any power was out of the question. The Henson family had a lot of power in this town and who knew how many hands they'd greased to keep their dirty deeds out of the public eye. I knew that from experience.

Telling Izzy might be an option, but I didn't know if telling her even more information about this situation I was involved in would put a larger target on her back.

"Are you still awake?"

I shook my head once before lifting my head and looking over at Izzy. She was now looking at me instead of at the stove. "Yeah? I think so."

Izzy chuckled at my indecisiveness. "Are you hungry? I'm making enough breakfast for two and it's almost ready."

My stomach chose that exact moment to growl. "Sounds like I am."

That wasn't a surprise either. I'd lost my appetite after my encounter with Nash and hadn't eaten dinner the night before. It was coming back to bite me in the ass now.

"Excellent. Then we can sit down and eat and you can tell me why you have that look on your face."

Of course, she noticed that something was wrong. Even with the time we spent apart, she still knew if something wasn't right in my world. "Fine. I'll grab some drinks from the fridge."

I stood up, slightly wobbly due to the lack of food in my system and walked over to the fridge. By the time I found cups and poured us two glasses of orange juice, Izzy made plates for both of us and set them on the dining room table.

Once the two of us sat down and had taken a few bites of our food, Izzy cleared her throat and said, "Now tell me what's wrong."

There was no doubt in her voice. She knew she was right. I knew that lying would only make me feel worse.

I couldn't stomach making up an excuse on the spot, so I told her the truth. "I ran into Nash at the library yesterday."

Her fork was midway between the plate and her mouth when she paused, and I was concerned she might drop the utensil. Izzy placed the fork back down on her plate before she said, "You've got to be kidding. The look on your face tells me that wasn't all that happened. Tell me everything."

Instead of doing what she requested right away, I took a sip from my orange juice to buy me precious seconds. I took a deep breath before placing the cup down on the table, and then I told her everything about what I remembered from yesterday. Izzy let me tell my version of events without interrupting, choosing to listen intently. Her eyes never left me, and when I finished telling the story, silence filled the space my voice had occupied.

That was until Izzy pushed her chair back and stood up. "I'm going to get him."

I was thankful for the burst of energy from the food I'd eaten and the orange juice I drank because it helped me to jump up and grab Izzy's arm. "You can't do that."

"The hell I can't. He touched you!"

"And you running over there to threaten him is only going to make things worse for me, and you know that."

If my actions hadn't stopped her, I knew my words would. When I was confident she wouldn't take off after Nash, I let her go and followed her lead as she sat back down in her seat.

"You're right. We must be more strategic about this and going over there would be a terrible idea."

I nodded my head, agreeing with this course of action over the one she initially wanted to go with. "I'm not sure what we can do about it if I'm being honest. What I do know is that we have to be careful no matter which way we turn because he's a part of the Henson family. Even if you don't count the family's connections, his father is the mayor of this town, for goodness' sake."

Izzy didn't say a word because she knew I was right. Who were we going to talk to about Nash harassing me? Star quarterback of Brentson University and the mayor's son.

"You know what makes matters worse?"

I raised an eyebrow at Izzy. How could anything be worse than this? "What's that?"

"I don't know how much you've kept up with the Henson family over the years, but supposedly, Van Henson is planning on running to become the next governor of New York. I wouldn't be surprised if that was a stepping-stone for him to run for president of the United States in the future. None of this has been confirmed yet, but I wouldn't be surprised if this was true."

Izzy was right and that made things worse. If Van Henson had bigger political ambitions than just staying in Brentson, then this could get really ugly. And the information I knew put my life in more danger than I'd imagined.

"Raven?"

I looked at Izzy before looking back down at the plate of food in front of me. I pushed the plate away from me and sighed. The food had barely been touched, but once again, my appetite had disappeared. "I'm not hungry again. I'll wrap this up and eat it later."

"Cling film is in that cabinet over there." She paused as I got up and followed her directions, and when I walked back over to the table with the cling film in my hand, she continued, "I'm sorry to have spoiled your appetite."

"It's not your fault. I'm glad you told me."

I meant those words and I set a mental reminder to myself to eat my food in about an hour or so. Without a doubt, I needed all of my strength and brain power to deal with what would be thrown at me. I knew this wasn't the end but the start of a war between me and the Henson family.

Izzy snapped her fingers, drawing my attention to her. We'd been watching a show while her other roommates were out doing who knows what, giving us the place to ourselves for the time being. It had brought me back to my childhood and the times she and I would spend over at each other's homes while we watched movies or a television show.

But I couldn't focus on the show we were binge watching. I was embarrassed that this was the second or third time today she'd caught me lost in a daydream. "There's something I hadn't mentioned to you earlier today. It's about Nash."

My heart skipped a beat, and I hated that the mere mention of his name had this effect on me. "What is it?"

"He's a member of the Chevaliers."

Her comment drew more questions than anything else. I

turned to look at her and asked, "The Chevaliers? What is that? Weird name."

Izzy shrugged. "It's not like I named them."

My eyes narrowed at her. "I know that."

She chuckled in return. "Anyway, I don't know much about them, other than them being very secretive and that there is a branch on Brentson's campus. A lot of rich and popular guys are involved in it and they..."

Based on her basic assessment, it did not surprise me that Nash was a member of the Chevaliers. But what worried me was Izzy's voice trailing off and her looking down at the ground. It seemed as if I wasn't the only one who was now distracted. I gave her a moment to figure out what she wanted to say and when she turned to look at me again, there was something about the look in her eyes... it was different.

"I've heard they've done some scary shit."

"What type of 'scary shit'?"

She rubbed a hand down the side of her face and then said, "A Brentson University student died mysteriously last year. Caleb was his name, and he was a freshman."

My eyebrows raised and my mouth dropped open involuntarily. "Wait what? Here? On campus?"

Izzy swallowed hard. "Yes."

"I don't remember seeing anything about that when I looked up Brentson before I drove here... then again, it was a year ago..."

Izzy crossed her arms over her chest, signaling to me that she wasn't comfortable talking about this. "Oh, there wasn't much information about it released when it happened either."

None of what she was saying made sense. How wouldn't a

student dying on campus make the front-page news locally at the very least?

"I'm not following this because none of it makes any sense and how it's related to this secret society..."

And that was when it clicked. Izzy also recognized when I figured it out because she gave me a knowing head nod. "You can't be serious. You think his death was related to the Chevaliers?"

"Will I say that in public? No. But between you and me..."

"Rewind for a second. What gave you this idea?"

"He was a freshman who was rumored to be one of their recruits. Nothing was confirmed and the student body was never told officially what happened. Student government even went to ask administrative officials about what happened and demanded that we deserved some answers, but they received none. It cast a dark cloud over the university and all of us here, but especially for those who knew him. I can't even imagine how his family is doing now, let alone when they first received the news."

Even with the prospect of bad press, Brentson University officials didn't care. If the connection between the Chevaliers and Caleb was true, it's obvious that up the chain of command, the Chevaliers must have some leverage to be able to bury this. But who were they?

10

NASH

I grunted as I exerted even more energy. I don't know what I'd been expecting when I'd read that leadership had selected me to take part in the Chevaliers leadership trials, but this wasn't it. I'd been here since 8:50 p.m. and while I didn't know exactly what time it was now, I suspected it had to be early morning the next day.

Standing out in the pouring rain in the dark while trying to navigate an obstacle course. The burning in my lungs as I ran to a wall, climbed up, and pulled myself over was more than I thought I would be experiencing. This made football practice and games look easy.

Thankfully, that was the last obstacle for me, and I ran back to the area where our leaders were waiting for us. I didn't care if I looked weak after throwing myself on the ground just a few feet away from where they were standing. If it made it easier for me to catch my breath, I was going to do it, no matter the optics.

"Good job, Henson."

All I did was nod and wave my hand, acknowledging that

I'd heard him but that I was in no shape to respond. Everything within me was pounding to the point where I didn't know which way was up. Water was dripping into my mouth, and I wasn't sure if it was sweat, tears, or rain. When I finally calmed my racing heart down a bit, I realized I was the only one who had finished. I was proud of the feat but also wondered if anyone else would survive and if not, what that would mean for these trials.

"Nash?"

I looked up and found Trevor, another member of the Chevaliers leadership standing in front of me. "Yes?"

"Come with me."

I stood up and followed Trevor back into the house. I was asked to wait in the living room with my head down so as not to look at the other men as they finished the course and filed into this room. The room had barely any light in it, and I knew that was done on purpose. It was a common theme that carried on throughout our meetings, but I couldn't help but wonder if the darkness was created to hide some of the embarrassment these men might have felt due to their performance this morning.

I don't know how long I waited there, but I didn't look up even as I heard people coming into the room. It took a few minutes, but then I finally heard Tomas speak.

"Do you know why you're here?"

Our chairman's voice echoed across the walls of the chamber. Although it was a question, no one answered because we weren't meant to. It was a rhetorical question. We all knew why we were here. The only response he received was the gasps of breath from several of the other members who were vying for the top prize. This time, I tried to keep my need for more air to myself, instead choosing to take deeper breaths quietly so as not to show any signs of weakness around my competitors.

I looked down at my feet as water dripped off my body. Being pushed through what was essentially a boot camp had wreaked havoc on our bodies. To make things even more difficult, we had to do it in the pouring rain.

Having to make our way through an obstacle course that tested our physical strength and durability was a wild card. I hoped the rest of these trials would be nothing compared to what we'd just gone through.

Tomas's words cut above the noisiness in the room once more. "If you don't, then you can walk out that fucking door right now. While you passed the initiation phase to become a Chevalier, it's clear that it is all you'll ever be and that is fine if you want to continue to be mediocre."

I knew he was full of shit with that line. No one who was recruited and became a member of the Chevaliers was mediocre in the slightest because the Chevaliers didn't recruit mediocre men. Now, if our chairman was judging us against those who weren't given the opportunity to start this competition, then maybe he was right.

"Bow. Down."

I glanced at the others in the room out of the corner of my eye before following the command. I assumed that they, too, had finished the obstacle course and did as instructed.

Between the candlelight and the cloaks the men in front of us wore, it was hard to get a read on their faces, but that was done on purpose. We weren't allowed to anticipate what was about to happen because anticipation would mean that we might gain an advantage. The whole point of this entire process was to keep us on our toes and be able to conquer whatever they threw at us. After all, that was meant to help prepare some of us to become the next leaders of the Chevaliers, and I wouldn't settle for anything less than the chairmanship.

For one, it was a leg up that I had on my father. When he'd attended Brentson, he, too, had been a part of the Chevaliers, much like his father before him and his father before him. But no one in my family had ever become chairman of the chapter.

I was determined to make that change this semester.

Each chairman for the next year was selected during the fall semester of their junior year and was expected to spend the following spring semester coming up to speed with the responsibilities that they would undertake during their senior year. The rigorous tests that we went through were supposed to weed the men out who weren't fit for the job. Some of them would become other members of the board, but that was a participation trophy to me.

I was determined to be the last man standing. I *would* be the last one standing.

"You all have done good work tonight. Not well, but good. I expect that our next meeting will be better."

"Yes, Chairman." We said the statement in unison, but I could still hear some trying to catch their breaths. *Fucking amateurs.*

"You each will receive an envelope on the way out of here. Open it when you get home alone. You will need to conquer whatever it is on that envelope to see if you're worthy enough to move on. Some of you will be surprised by what you'll find.

Some of you will not be. Congratulations on even making it this far. You've been dismissed."

"Thank you, Chairman."

Those of us who were bowing our heads waited until the men in front of us had left the room before looking up. When I was sure that our leaders had left the room, I turned to look around and found varying expressions on the faces of the men around me. While no one uttered a word, it was easy to see that most looked exhausted and scared. Good. That should hopefully make this easier than expected. That was until my eyes landed on Landon Brennan.

Landon's face was stoic, not portraying any emotion, and that didn't come as a shock to me. I viewed him as my greatest competitor out of the seven other men here, and when his eyes met mine, I could see that he thought the same. I dipped my head slightly, acknowledging that I saw him before taking my place in line to exit the room.

We were greeted by an usher as we left the room and one by one. Trevor handed each man a black envelope with what I assumed would be gold lining, similar to the one I'd received when I was first invited to join the Chevaliers and the one I'd gotten when I was informed I was being invited to take part in this.

As soon as the envelope was in my possession, the figurative weight of it caused my hand to drop to my side. The men that I was competing with were only half the battle. What was inside this envelope was the other half.

I grabbed my things that I had left in a pile in the front hall and exited the building. Of course, by the time I left, the rain had slowed and just a slight drizzle greeted me. I didn't take another deep breath until I was locked inside of my car and pulled out of the long driveway that led to Chevalier Manor.

The tension in my body eased the more distance I put between myself and what had just occurred. Even after everything I'd just done, there would be no resting for me because my day was just beginning. Football practice began in about an hour and a half and I only had to make it through that because my only class for today was canceled. I'd already made plans to crash after practice was done.

Although I would never admit it out loud, Raven was still on my mind. The ritual that we'd performed should have been at the forefront, but my thoughts kept drifting back to her. I drove back to my apartment with the envelope we received at the end of the ritual burning a hole in my passenger seat. It reminded me of another letter I'd received years ago and a similar drive I'd made. Both would be forever etched in my memory.

I snuck in through the back entrance of my building because I didn't want to deal with seeing my doorman or the person who'd gotten stuck working the late-night-early-morning shift at the front desk.

The elevator ride seemed to take longer than usual, but it could have been because of the anticipation that had been building within me as I wondered what could be written on the envelope I was holding.

I didn't open the envelope until I was alone in my apartment, not that I had come across many people on the journey back home anyway. Before I sat down to open it, I grabbed some water to hydrate after a long early morning with nothing to drink.

After I took a long sip of water, I put my glass down and

opened the envelope. I could hear my heart pounding in my ears as the paper ripped beneath my fingers and I wondered what my test would be. I needed to prove that I was committed to the Chevaliers no matter what and I was ready to do so, no matter the cost.

Others had told me about what types of things had been written in their envelopes, although no one confirmed to me exactly what had been written. I didn't blame them, because a lot of them contained deep dark secrets that they'd hoped would never see the light of day.

But it seemed as if our leaders had already known. They knew me better than I knew myself.

Because when I saw Raven Goodwin listed on the piece of paper I was holding, I shouldn't have been shocked. I was convinced this was why she was brought back here in the first place.

I now knew that everything surrounding my ascension to the next chairman of the Chevaliers' Brentson University chapter would revolve around owning my greatest enemy, but one that used to be my greatest temptation: her.

11

RAVEN

"You're coming out with us, if it's the last thing I do."

I sighed and closed my eyes, not wanting to hear Izzy's arguments about why I needed to go out and party with them tonight. I could think of a million reasons why I shouldn't go to this party, but Izzy's instance was peer pressuring me to go out and have fun with her and our roommates, Lila and Erika. Deep down, I knew it might be an opportunity to get to know Lila and Erika who had become slightly more friendly toward me. Strong emphasis on slightly, however.

I opened my eyes and stared down at my lap. Before I could respond, Izzy wasted no time in launching into another reason why I should be getting dressed right now instead of picking the lint off of my black yoga pants.

"It's Saturday night and you've had a long, long week. It's time you got out there and let loose. Experience more of what college life is about."

She'd made another fine argument. It had been a long week where I spent most of my time trying to find places to do my homework that were quiet and didn't involve me running into a six-foot, three-inch-tall quarterback that was out for my blood. Or so it seemed.

Thankfully, it had worked, and I hadn't run into Nash at all since the incident at the library.

"Plus it helps get you prepped for my twenty-first birthday party."

That forced me out of my own head enough to side-eye her. "Why the hell do I need to get prepped for anything?"

"Because it's going to be a weekend-long extravaganza and best of all, we won't be here on campus."

Why did I agree to do whatever she wanted for her twenty-first birthday? "Where are we going?"

"To New York City! But more on that later. Are you going to come?"

With a heavy sigh, I stood up, ready to admit defeat. "Fine, I'll come with you."

Izzy's squeal made me shake my head. Who knew someone would be this excited about dragging someone else to a party?

"Do you need anything to wear? I have plenty of things you can borrow."

I knew she did and while we weren't the same size, I would be surprised if she didn't have something in there that I could turn into an outfit worthy enough of going out in. Once I'd taken a quick shower, I walked into my bedroom and found that Izzy had laid out a couple of tops that I could choose from for tonight. I decided on a navy top that showed a bit more cleavage than I normally would and chose a pair of black jeans and boots that I'd already owned. I took my time brushing out my hair to buy me time from having to face Izzy in the living room. Then again, she would have no problem coming back into my room and dragging me out if that was what it took.

Before she could string that idea together, I grabbed my wallet and shut off my light as I walked out of my bedroom. Izzy, Lila, and Erika all turned to look at me as I entered the living room and I saw the sign of approval in what I chose to wear in their eyes.

"There you are. Are you ready to go?"

"I guess so."

I COULDN'T REMOVE the smile that was currently plastered on my face even if I tried. I was grinning from ear to ear as I made my way to grab another beer from a cooler. While I hadn't had too much to drink in my life, I was fully aware that the beer I was trying to get tasted like absolute shit, but I didn't care. This had to be one of the best nights of my life.

Izzy, Lila, Erika, and I had party hopped and ended up at one of Brentson University's fraternity houses. I don't know what I'd been expecting when we got here, but it wasn't this. The party that they were hosting seemed to be happening on all three levels of the house and we were currently living it up in the basement. It had been turned into a dance floor and right now was currently the best option we had. Outside of getting a fake ID for Izzy, we didn't have the option of going to any of the bars or clubs in town unless Izzy didn't want to come with. Since she'd organized the whole thing, that wouldn't be fair to her at all.

When I arrived back to my group, Izzy couldn't control

her giggles. It was obvious she was having a fantastic night right along with me.

Izzy was right. Being able to spend time away, not thinking about all the shit I needed to get done, had been the right choice for me.

"Psssttt."

After hearing the drawn-out noise, I turned to find Izzy smiling at me. The glassy look in her eyes made me shake my head. If that had been her attempt at whispering, she was going to be in rough shape the next morning.

"What's up?"

"I think Landon is trying to get your attention."

"Who?"

"The guy over there with the dark T-shirt on," she said as she pointed.

I would have probably told her to be a little more inconspicuous under any other circumstances but given that I could see that she was tipsier than I was, I knew that would be pointless.

I turned to look over my shoulder and found three guys standing on the other side of the room. The guy in the dark T-shirt was staring me down and I could feel my cheeks starting to warm. It had been so long since I'd paid attention to anyone having even the slightest interest in me that him just looking at me was enough to make me nervous. My thoughts briefly veered back to the last person who had bestowed any interest in me and the last time I'd seen him was when he'd grabbed me and threatened me. I bit my lip and looked down as I thought about Nash.

"He's headed our way!"

Shit. At least with the loud music playing, there was a

chance that he hadn't heard. I guess he'd taken my action as an incentive to come over here. Then again, would talking to another guy be the worst thing in the world?

I looked up when he was only a few feet away and gave him a small smile and leaned forward so that we could hear him.

"Hey." It was all he said, but it made Izzy giggle. His eyes never strayed from me. "I would offer to get you a drink, but I noticed you just returned from getting one."

Izzy leaned toward us and said, "But I could hold that for her while you ask her to dance."

I couldn't help but roll my eyes up to the ceiling. This was so out of hand, but I was also thankful she didn't just spit out that we should go to the corner and make out or something along those lines.

As if the DJ, who I was pretty sure was a member of the fraternity that was hosting this party if the letters on his shirt were anything to go by, heard what Izzy had said, the current song blended into a more upbeat track that would make it much easier for anyone to dance to.

"Want to?"

I nodded and handed my drink to Lila. "Hold this and make sure she doesn't drink it."

"Hey!" Izzy shouted before hitting me harder than necessary on the shoulder. "Go!"

I looked at Erika and motioned to Izzy, telling her to keep an eye on her just in case. I hadn't gotten a chance to open it anyway so if the drink somehow found its way into Izzy's hands, it would be easy to tell. Once I was satisfied that everything with the girls was taken care of, I followed him.

It wasn't as obvious when we were standing on the

outskirts of the dance floor, but once you were in the thick of it, the amount of body heat that surrounded you was all that you could feel. People either grinding up on each other or making out was all that you could see. This had never been my scene outside of prom and a couple of high school parties, but I was now determined to experience what I'd missed.

"You know I don't even know your name." That line sounded cheesy to even my ear.

"It's Landon," he whispered in my ear. "And yours?"

I didn't want to be cocky, but him not knowing my name after all the stares I first got when I arrived was a relief. In fact, while walking into the parties we stopped by tonight, having no one bat an eyelash at me brought on a sense of comfort, but maybe that was the booze talking.

"I'm Raven," I said as I tucked my hair behind my ear.

"Well it's nice to meet you, Raven."

His voice tickled my ear and the sensation made me grin. While I wasn't desperate for attention, I had to admit that being the center of someone else's gaze felt good in this moment. His hands found my waist and I looked down at his hands touching my body. As we moved to the beat, something about the energy in the room shifted for me. The gentle buzz I had going faded, and I wasn't sure why.

I looked up, and then I found the reason for the change, and he was storming toward us. It was as if my body had sensed that he was here. Landon must have seen him coming too because he stopped moving and once again, I felt as if the vibe in the room had shifted and all eyes were on me.

"What are you doing here?" Nash's question was more of a demand than anything else. Landon shifted his body so that he was between Nash and me. It was a chivalrous move, but I was also worried about him. While I didn't know anything about Nash anymore, I could easily read the look in his eyes. It said that if anyone got in his way, he had no problem using any means necessary to get what he wanted.

I could smell the alcohol on his breath, but nothing about his demeanor showed that he was under the influence. His darkened stare as he waited for my response left me stunned. All of the words I wanted to say, about how he had no right to do this and that he needed to fuck off, died on my lips. It took a few seconds before I was able to find my words again.

I moved out of Landon's shadow because I wasn't afraid of Nash. If he wanted to attempt to be a bully, I wasn't going to cower behind someone else in response. "Minding my own business, which you can't seem to do. Don't you have something else more important to do besides bothering us?" *Real smooth, Raven.*

"Come with me."

"Absolutely not. Fuck off." There were the words.

"I said, come with me." This time Nash grabbed my arm, not enough to hurt me but his grip was tight enough that it would be very difficult for me to get out of his grasp.

"Shouldn't you be doing something else? Like preparing?"

Nash ignored him and said nothing.

"Look, Nash—"

Nash turned to Landon who'd just uttered those words. "I'm not talking to you."

"And I'm not going anywhere with you," I chimed in.

Nash stared down Landon long enough to make me think there might be some shared history there and that this might not be completely about me. When Nash turned his head toward me, the smirk he gave me was reminiscent of the boy that I used to know. That was, before it turned wicked.

"Wouldn't it be tragic for this fucker to die all because he dared to touch you?"

I watched Landon adjust his stance out of the corner of my eye and I couldn't blame him. I didn't know about Landon, but if I'd just gotten threatened by a guy who was slightly taller, looked to outweigh me, was athletic as fuck, and rumored to be a member of an organization that didn't have any problems with killing people, I would be shaking. Landon however looked like he might be willing to take Nash on.

"What in the entire—"

I heard Izzy's statement and when Nash looked in her direction, silence followed. I assume either Lila or Erika held her back and it was probably for the best. The last thing I wanted was for her to end up being hurt. Nash turned his attention back to me.

"Did you make a decision?"

Nash's question cut through me like a knife. I swallowed hard. I didn't know if he was talking about me stepping outside or Landon and him getting into a fist fight. "Landon, I'm going to step outside with him, but I'll be right back."

"Are you sure about this? I don't want him to—"

"Want me to what?" Nash took another step toward him, and I placed my hand on Nash's chest in an attempt to stop him from advancing on Landon.

"Forget what he said. I already agreed to step outside with you, but I'm not going any farther than the yard of this house unless you want to add kidnapping to the list of crimes you've committed tonight."

I watched as a tic started in Nash's jaw after my comment and if he wasn't happy before he approached me, he really wasn't happy now. But that didn't seem to deter him from his main mission. He spared one last glance at me before he stalked away, I assumed expecting me to follow.

"I'm sorry, Landon," I whispered before I took a deep breath and followed him with a trail of stares in my wake.

Word must have spread about what was going on downstairs because once I reached the landing, I could feel everyone's eyes on me. While I hated to be the center of attention, I refused to bow down under the pressure that was laid on me. I kept my head up high as I followed Nash out the front door of the fraternity.

When he came to a stop, I had to admit that I was shocked that he paused just before the fraternity house's yard ended, following the parameters that I set.

At first, he kept his back toward me. When he made no moves to speak, I sucked my teeth and shook my head. He just wanted to waste my time.

It wasn't until I spoke that he turned around. "What the hell do you want?"

"I want to play a little game."

His response forced me to do a double take. There was no way that I heard him correctly. "Excuse me. You want to do what?"

"I want to play a little game."

I folded my arms across my chest because this was ridiculous. "So, I heard you correctly. Since I'm not interested in whatever you're trying to do, I'm going to leave now."

As I spun on my heel and took a step away from him, I heard him say, "It's in your best interest to stay right here."

Anger that had already been bubbling under the surface because of his actions was creeping up, threatening me with the thought that I might lose my cool. If it happened, I knew that I would say something that I couldn't take back. Then again, did I really care?

He spoke again before I could say anything. "I'm not kidding, Raven. You already walked away from me once, and now the stakes are much higher."

The low blow he sent my way hurt more than I expected. Was he still hurt by me leaving? Even if he was, it did little to calm the anger I was feeling. I whipped my body around to face him again. "Oh really? What are the stakes?"

I knew I'd given in and that I was right where he wanted me to be. I hated it, but now I needed to know what he was getting at.

"In order to keep your little secret quiet, there's something I want you to do for me."

I almost laughed in his face. "Hell no. That literally makes no sense. Everyone has this preconceived notion that they know what I did, so there's nothing else you can do that would make it any worse."

That wicked smile was back on his face. It looked scarier with the streetlight reflecting off of the sharp edges of his face. The same face I used to hold in my hands as we kissed in his car outside of my childhood home. "That's not the secret I'm referring to."

I knew my confusion was written all over my face. I had no idea what he was talking about, so he continued. "Goodwin, now we both know that's not true."

Hearing my last name on his lips once again did anything but bring me warm and fuzzy feelings. It dragged my anger out even more and I refused to rein it in as it came kicking and screaming to the surface. "Stop calling me that."

This time, Nash chuckled. "It's your name, isn't it? Or were you lying about that shit too?"

I rolled my eyes at him. "Give me a fucking break."

"Like you gave me one? Anyway, it's not like any of this matters because you don't have a say. I can call you whatever I want and do whatever I want and you're just going to have to grin and bear it. You don't want all the things that you've done to my family to get out. We both know that what this fucking town knows is just the tip of the iceberg."

That was when it hit me. Ice filled my veins as realization set in. I knew exactly what he was talking about. "You wouldn't dare."

Nash shrugged like he hadn't just dropped a bomb on my life. "I owe no allegiance to you. If it just so happens to get out, then it does."

"You are a disgusting, childish piece of shit."

"Feeling is mutual, sweetheart."

Although it was cool outside, I could feel the temperature in my body shifting. My anger was steadily increasing, causing my body to feel as if I'd had a fever that was trying to break. I had to get away from him.

As if he could read my thoughts, Nash took a step closer to me and rubbed his knuckles against my face. I revolted against his touch and moved away from it. It only made his smile deepen.

"You're going to receive a text with an address. Be there at nine p.m. tomorrow."

"That's not sketchy at all. And if I don't go?"

"Your secret will no longer be one, Goodwin."

He tried to touch my face again, but this time I was prepared and didn't let him. He shook his head slightly before walking away from me, leaving me alone and staring after him.

I wished I'd never come back here. I knew nothing good would come of it.

"Are you okay?"

I turned and found Izzy, Lila, and Erika walking toward me. Izzy's mood had changed, and I knew that the time between when she'd sent me to dance with Landon and now had led to her sobering up. I could see the guilt all over her face. She'd been the one who'd asked me multiple times to go out with her, but it hadn't been her fault that Nash had arrived and acted the way that he did.

"I think so, but I'm ready to go home."

"Okay, let's go."

12

RAVEN

My fingers flew over my phone screen as I typed my next inquiry into the ever-present saga related to Nash. Izzy had told me about what she knew about the Chevaliers, but it wasn't much. All it had done was leave me with more questions than answers. Since I'd arrived outside of Nash's apartment way too early, I decided to burn some time by doing some quick research.

That was, if I could find anything.

My search proved to be somewhat fruitless. There wasn't much to find about them on the internet. There was a website that mentioned they were a secret society but didn't have much else. It was as if the society had taken special precautions to not be discovered. But why?

Sure, being a secret society implied that they needed to remain confidential, but having barely any mentions online was strange. What kind of organization was this?

Before I could spiral further, I put my phone away. I realized I still had several minutes to wait until nine. I stared at the clock on my car's dashboard as the time dwindled down.

The numbers on the clock, 8:54 p.m., were like a spotlight on what was about to come. It was Sunday evening, and it was closing in on the time that Nash asked me to meet with him.

The text message that had been sitting in my inbox since last night was at the forefront of my mind as I contemplated my choices.

Choices? That was a funny thought.

I didn't really have an option here. I could have chosen not to go, but the ramifications would be too great. With most things, I didn't care what people thought about me. Most people had already formed a lot of opinions about me, but I didn't want this to get out. At least, this wasn't the way I'd planned on having it come out.

Because in this town, nothing stayed a secret for too long.

This was why I was sitting outside of this luxury apartment building where my ex-boyfriend held my fate in his hands.

This wasn't how I thought things would go. I'd known there was always a chance I would run into Nash because Brentson, while a decent-sized town, still felt too small at times. It didn't help that we were going to the same university now too, and part of me wondered if that had all been by design. What I hadn't expected was to be thrown into this position, where he held all the cards and I had none.

I bit the corner of my lip before I turned the engine off. There was no point in waiting any longer, because I was just delaying the inevitable. I locked my car door and walked toward the building. I'd hoped I would have another moment to myself before I had to face Nash, but he was waiting for me in the lobby.

It pained me to look at him and think about our shared

history. Every time thoughts of him appeared, I couldn't help but remember the good times we spent together. But when he looked at me with those blue eyes that I fell in love with when we were kids, I saw nothing but hatred. That was enough to sober anyone's feelings about this situation up.

He nodded his head at me as I approached him, acknowledging me, but the look in his eyes remained the same. To anyone else standing in this lobby, it would appear that we were cordial, and I knew we had them fooled. Because whatever Nash had planned for me would be anything but. It felt as if I were walking into the lion's den. There would be carnage as a result, and I could only imagine I would be the one left picking up the mental pieces of whatever he'd left me in.

We walked toward the elevator and rode up to his floor in silence. When he led me into his apartment, I couldn't help but think how different it was from anything I'd ever seen. It was almost like something you would see on a television show that was trying to be relatable and failed. The apartment was a dream for anyone of any age to live in but to live in something like this during college while the rest of us couldn't afford anything close to this was eye-opening.

I'd known that the Henson family was very wealthy when I was dating Nash in high school. It hadn't been a big secret since I'd gotten invited to several of the parties and functions they'd held at their home because of Nash's father's involvement in politics. The chip that his dad had on his shoulder about me was because of my social status.

Money hadn't grown on trees for me. We were never without and thankfully, always had a roof over our heads because my grandparents paid off the home that they later left to my mother, who then willed it down to me. But even when my mom was alive and my net worth hadn't grown significantly due to inheriting a home, Van Henson never cared for me.

But Nash and I hadn't cared. The only thing that mattered was us. Until it didn't.

Over the years, I realized how much I hadn't belonged in their world; a world that could fix any problem by throwing money at it, where I wasn't afforded the same luxury. I sort of tried to use that angle to my advantage and lost. It's why I left this town as if I was trying to outrun a storm that was bearing down, prepared to strike at any minute.

The storm had been in my heart because my secret forced me to leave Nash behind. And now here I was, staring back at him while he looked as if he wouldn't even spit on me if I was on fire.

"Sit down."

I hadn't expected him to be a decent host and ask me if I wanted a drink when I walked into his apartment. He didn't even bother.

"I'd rather stand."

He shrugged, clearly not giving a fuck. "Suit yourself."

I followed him with my eyes as he took a seat on his couch, looking as relaxed as ever. It was as if he wasn't about to say some things that might ruin everything I had going for me. "I think it's time that I inform you about my little game."

I walked over to the wall on the far side of the room and leaned against it. It would have looked strange to the casual observer, but that didn't matter. We were alone, as far as I could see, and I needed to put as much distance between us as possible.

When my eyes met his, the tension in the room increased tenfold. I tried not to show the nervousness that had formed in my belly as I waited for him to speak. Whatever he was going to say, I wouldn't like, and it made sense to just get it over with as quickly as possible.

"There are quite a few things I missed out on in high school."

That was not where I thought he was going with this.

"What the—what the hell are you talking about?"

"I'm not going to lie to you, Goodwin. You truly had me fucked up when we were kids. You left me on the day we graduated from high school standing there with just a note that had no explanation. Only that you were sorry."

I fought to control the eye roll I wanted to throw his way at him, emphasizing the word "lie." Instead, I studied him as I tried to come to terms with what he was saying. What he was saying or the matter in which he was saying it made no sense to me. Nash being under the influence passed through my mind, but I shoved the thought away. He seemed very in control, even if he was talking in what felt like a huge riddle.

As my irritation with him grew, I sighed to relieve some of the tension. "I don't know what you're talking about."

"I would have done anything for you. All you had to do was ask for it, and I would have given you the whole damn world."

I swallowed hard to hide my emotions. I knew that was true. He would have hung the damn moon for me if I'd told him that was what I wanted.

But I wasn't the only one trying to hold it together. That control that I'd seen in Nash just a moment ago? It seemed to be slipping away the more he brought up our past. Flashes of fire in his eyes appeared, and I knew I was walking on a proverbial tightrope between both of our emotions. I didn't know the dangers that lay below if I slipped and tumbled into the shadows.

Being cautious with Nash was the smart approach, but something within me refused to do it. I wanted to fight him every step of the way. "Can you spit it out so I can get out of here and move on with my life?"

"If I call you, you drop whatever it is you're doing, and you come to me. If you don't, there will be punishments. You keep disobeying me and I have no problem leaking what I know about you."

"Is this your version of blackmailing me?" It was ironic, given what I'd done to his father. "Absolutely fucking not."

Nash stood up and walked over to where I was standing. I regretted leaning against the wall in his living room because now I had nowhere to go and nowhere to hide. Any sense of the courage I'd had was gone about as quickly as it had taken Nash to walk across the room.

He stuck his finger under my chin and lifted my head so that I was staring up into his eyes. This time, however, his eyes weren't focused on mine. They were staring at my lips.

I was stunned that he was touching me again after all these years. His touch dredged up memories of the happy times that we spent together.

"You don't mean any of that. I bet under this mask you have on, you're freaking the fuck out because if your little secret gets out, you're done. Or you could just leave town, and all of this will go away."

I watched the challenge form in his eyes. The corner of his lip twitched before I snatched my head away from his touch. It was as if he'd burned me. His words had the same effect as a flamethrower blowing on me. "You thought this all out, didn't you? I'm not leaving town."

Nash's lips formed a smirk before he raised an eyebrow at me. It was as if he expected that would have been my answer. "What's keeping you here?"

There was no chance in hell that I was telling him anything. "That's none of your business."

"Then you only have one choice."

I took a deep breath and sighed because he was right as much as I hated to admit it. "What types of things do you want me to do if I were to agree to your little 'game'?"

"That's for me to know and you'll be informed when you're needed."

The urge to tell him to fuck off was strong, but I knew I couldn't. I needed to remain at Brentson until further notice and Nash wasn't about to keep me from completing my goal. Finding out what happened to my mother went above anything and everything Nash could ever do to me.

I'd made the decision to play his little game, but there was one thing he would never have again: my heart.

13

NASH

"Does anyone have any more business that needs to be brought to our attention?"

The barely lit room was silent with mostly candles providing the light that we had. The silence caused the mood in the room to shift. I was willing to bet that everyone in here was happy that this meeting was over so we could leave. It was a Friday, and no one wanted to be stuck in a meeting when we could do other things.

"Hearing none. This afternoon's meeting is adjourned."

Someone turned up the lights while a couple of other men walked over to pull up the window blinds. As the Chevaliers meeting ended, my eyes met Landon's across the room. It was the first time I'd seen him since the incident with Raven at the frat house. He dipped his head at me, acknowledging my presence. We still had unfinished business about Raven, but that would have to wait until I finished what I was doing here.

I watched as everyone but leadership stood up, prepared to file out of the room, and go on with the rest of their day. I loosened my tie and stayed seated as I waited for the room to empty. It was a requirement for us to wear suits and ties to official meetings, but once the meeting was over, all bets were off.

This impromptu meeting had occurred because of a last-minute provision that we needed to vote on. The easiest option to get this done was to have everyone come in this afternoon if you didn't have class for a short period of time and vote to pass or fail the stipulation.

I sat before them, waiting for the chairman to speak. As their eyes bore into mine, I couldn't help but feel slightly uncomfortable. I knew they were doing it on purpose, but I refused to show any emotion to indicate I was feeling as such.

"You received your envelope."

"Yes, I have." I recalled that the piece of paper in my envelope had indicated that I needed to conquer Raven Goodwin.

I was slowly becoming convinced that having her name written on the paper was fate. Another thing I needed to conquer before I could take my rightful place as the head of the Chevaliers. It was fitting that the three equal chambers of our organization were named after birds: Owl, Eagle, and Sparrow. When I was initiated into the Chevaliers, I became one of the Eagles because of strength and loyalty to the organization. Those that had become Owls were known for being wise, and Sparrows were known for being hardworking and caring.

In order to become chairman of the Chevaliers, I needed to demonstrate properties from all three chambers, and I was determined to do so.

"I would like to ask a question." Normally, I tried to be

respectful of our leaders and their time, but I needed to have the answer to this question.

Chairman Tomas nodded, so I asked my question. "Why Raven Goodwin?"

"Why *not* Raven Goodwin?"

Fair enough.

"But she hasn't been involved in my life in so long. Why would I need to conquer her?"

Tomas just stared at me as a hint of a smile played on his lips. I waited a couple of beats to see if he would answer my question, but when he didn't, I knew I had my answer.

I cleared my throat and asked, "Do you know why she returned?" It was the one thing I'd yet to figure out. I'd only asked to have one question answered, and I knew I was pushing the line here, but it had been bothering me the most.

When no one on the panel answered my question immediately, it was easy for me to reach a conclusion. They knew why she was here, but they had no reason to tell me now.

The Chevaliers acted on a need-to-know basis. If they didn't think you needed to know something, then you didn't know. And because I wasn't the current chairman or on the board of the society, I didn't have the privilege of knowing because they didn't deem it necessary.

"Maybe she, like you, received a calling to be here. In this place, at this exact time."

I was shocked that I'd received an answer at all. I didn't bother asking for more information because I knew it was all I was going to get. His pause was a full stop that left no more room for questioning. Raven's reappearance in my life remained a mystery, but I was determined to get to the bottom of it.

I nodded, silently thanking the men before me and walked away. My thoughts swirled about what this could mean, but that all came to a halt when I saw Landon. My mind immediately blanked out and I stalked over to him.

His smirk greeted me, and it took all of my self-control to not wipe it off his face. Instead of causing a scene in front of other Chevaliers who were hanging around after the meeting, I pulled Landon to the side. The only thing stopping me from punching him in the face right there was the leadership trials weighing heavy on my mind and the portrait of Virgil Cross looking down at me.

"What do you want, Henson?"

"Stay away from Goodwin."

"Who is..." Recognition flashed in his eyes. "Raven? From last weekend?"

I stared at him, and he crossed his arms.

"She seemed to be fair game last time I—"

"Stay away from her or I will fucking kill you. No questions asked."

His expression turned angry, and it was obvious he didn't take to kindly to my threat.

"I've been nice to you because I don't want to start any shit, but you aren't going to dictate who I can and cannot talk to."

"But I can, and I will."

Landon glared at me, I assumed in an attempt to intimidate me, but it had no effect. "Fuck right off, Henson. You're not going to do shit; you don't want to start any trouble because of leadership trials."

I brushed off his doubts about what I would and wouldn't do. "If I were you, I would take my warning seriously. I would hate to see you with a slit in your throat at the end of the day."

He couldn't contain the fear I saw briefly in his eyes. *Good.*

Having enough of this sparring match that wasn't much of a match to begin with, I walked away from him. I walked down the long hallway that was full of history. Leaders who had come before me or had steered this organization through good times and bad. The amount of history on these walls and the legacy these men left was unsurmountable. I briefly glanced at Damien Cross before continuing. He'd been chairman during his tenure at Brentson University and I admired what I knew about him.

As I stepped out of the Chevaliers Manor, I took off my suit jacket and walked out to my car. It was a rare Friday where I had nothing else to do that evening, outside of preparing for tomorrow's football game. A smirk appeared on my face as I realized it was an excellent opportunity to start my game with Raven. It would provide... a lot of stimulation ahead of our matchup.

No matter what I did, I couldn't get out of my mind the way she looked when I told her that she would be mine to do whatever I wanted to. I couldn't deny that her defiance was a huge turn on. The anger and grit she felt was something that shot a thrill through my entire body yet landed at my cock.

I meant what I said when I mentioned that there were several things I had missed out on in high school because I hadn't gotten enough of her. Now, I am determined to collect.

And it would include taming her.

As I pulled out of the parking lot of Chevalier Manor, my ringtone played. I didn't bother pulling my cell phone out because I knew it was a text, instead choosing to read the message on my car's dashboard.

Unknown Number: ***R is in New York City, celebrating a birthday. Thought you might want to check out a famous club that begins with the letter E.***

It was the same number that had texted me when I was sitting outside of Raven's apartment after the incident between her and me in the library. I'd done my due diligence to figure out who the hell it was but had come up empty. I hadn't bothered asking the Chevaliers about it either because even if it was connected to them in some way, they wouldn't admit to it.

No. There was a reason I knew this information, and I needed to act on it.

"Maybe she, like you, received a calling to be here. In this place, at this exact time."

Tomas's words ran through my head repeatedly. There was a reason why things were working out the way they were right now, and I should embrace it.

The text included enough hints about where she was, and based on my own research and deductions, I knew whose birthday she was celebrating. It might take me a bit to get there and set up what I wanted, but I knew exactly where I was going and what I needed to do.

"What's up, dude?"

"Are you up for going to New York City in a couple of hours?"

Easton didn't answer right away. "You know we have a football game tomorrow?"

I chuckled. "Since when do you like following the rules? I

promise to have us at our game with plenty of time to spare, just bring everything you need with you."

"You make an excellent point..." His voice trailed off before he said, "Okay, I'm game."

I couldn't fight my smile. Raven wanted to go out and party? Then we could go out and party.

14

RAVEN

"How the hell did you manage to get us in here?"

"Pleaded and begged my parents to see if they knew anyone who could get us in. And they somehow pulled this off. I can't believe it myself. By the way, that dress looks better on you than it ever did on me."

The light blue mini dress I'd selected from Izzy's closet was out of the norm for me, but this wasn't a normal weekend. I felt the need to change things up, and I'd accomplished that. Yes, I'd also been chilly on the way over here, but it was well worth it for how good I felt. I looked down at myself and wondered if she'd snuck some drinks while we weren't looking. We'd done a couple of shots before arriving at Elevate to help us get looser. And I was still blown that we were here.

Elevate was the epitome of a classy establishment. It had a sleek black, gray, and gold theme throughout the bar. I'd seen the atmosphere of the bar and dance floor change by switching the music and the lighting. One minute, it looked like a rave, and the next, it looked romantic with the lights turned low and soft music playing.

After Izzy had told Lila, Erika, and me she'd rented a fancy hotel room that overlooked parts of Manhattan and that we were going to Elevate to celebrate her birthday, I did my research. Getting into one of the most exclusive clubs in New York City was no small feat, especially for a twenty-first birthday party. Thank you, Mr. and Mrs. Deacon.

What no one had mentioned was that this place also had a sex club in the basement. While I had no plans to explore it, I found the idea of it interesting.

But here we were, sitting in one of the VIP areas, enjoying all the amenities that Elevate had to offer. I was grooving to the beat of the music when I felt my purse vibrate. I immediately knew it was my phone and that it more than likely was a text message.

Nash: ***My apartment. One hour.***

My heart stopped as a mixture of emotions flooded me. First, seeing his name appear on my screen jerked me back in time. Second, there was no way I could get back to Brentson in time.

How dare he only give me an hour's notice? Anger and annoyance pushed all of my other emotions by the wayside, and I sent him a curt text in return.

Me: ***I'm busy. We can discuss this later.***

I hoped my frustration with him was apparent, but I knew a lot could get lost in translation through text. I placed my phone back in my bag with plans to ignore it for the time being.

That plan was turned on its head when my phone vibrated again. With a sigh, I opened my bag up and maneuvered my phone so that I could see who it was without pulling my phone out of my purse. His name, in big letters, shined on my screen. I rolled my eyes as I ended the call. He could wait because he wasn't about to ruin Izzy's birthday for me.

"Raven?"

I looked up at Lila and gave her a big smile. It probably looked fake, but I didn't care. I was faking it until I made it.

"We're about to order drinks. Do you want anything?"

"A margarita would be great," I said. I looked around before I asked, "Where are Izzy and Erika?"

"Bathroom."

This time, I playfully rolled my eyes. Once you went to the bathroom, you risked having to go a million times. I knew it was only a matter of time before I had to go too.

I looked around the room and landed on a couple of guys in dark suits on the other side of VIP. One of them was looking at me curiously, and I couldn't help but feel slightly uncomfortable as he stared at me, but he made no moves to approach so I assumed I was safe.

A slight commotion drew my attention to the stairs, and I saw Izzy and Erika making their way back up the stairs with Izzy giggling. She was attempting to right the crown and the sash that we'd bought her to wear tonight, and it looked comical at best. She did a little jig as she sat back down in her seat just as our server for the night walked up with our drinks.

"I'll pay for it," I announced and reached into my purse to pull out some dollar bills.

The server shook her head. "No need. It's been taken care of for you."

"By whom?"

"He wished to remain anonymous."

What the fuck?

It took a few seconds for me to put it together, but I turned to see if I could find the man in the dark suit who had been staring in our direction only moments ago. But he was gone.

"Um, okay." After our server handed each of us our drinks, I waited until the girls were distracted before I leaned over and said, "Can I ask you to do something special for me?"

"Sure. What do you need?"

I whispered what I wanted to do and handed her a few bills. I watched as she gave me a big smile and confirmed that she would do as I requested. When our server walked away, I tried to swallow back the worry I felt about what had just happened and focused my attention on Izzy and everyone else. I slowly shook off the feeling and enjoyed the drink in front of me. The music that was playing throughout the club gave me the opportunity to shake off any worries that I'd had and get lost in the music. This might have been the most fun I'd had in forever.

I noticed our server before anyone else did and I couldn't fight my grin. This was perfect. I tapped Izzy on the shoulder and pointed toward the stairs that our server had just reached.

Her eyes immediately lit up like saucers. Our server was walking over with a miniature cake that had candles in it. It was a great idea because all of us had been drinking and maybe eating a little something would help soak up some of the alcohol.

We all sang happy birthday and watched as Izzy blew out her candles. Our server brought the cake back into the back before returning with equally cut slices of the cake for the four of us and the rest boxed up to take back to the hotel. When I finished my slice, I rose and adjusted my dress.

"I'm going to head to the bathroom," I said to Lila. She was probably the most sober, besides me, and that was confirmed when Izzy let out a scream that was almost ear piercing. I shook my head as I grabbed my purse and walked away with my ears slightly ringing from her yelling.

The bathroom in VIP was taken, so I headed downstairs to use one of the bathrooms that was reserved for the general population. There was no way I was going to be able to hold it. Thankfully, they had more stalls and there was no wait. I washed my hands and quickly put some more lipstick on. I studied myself in the mirror and knew I looked damn good. Maybe I could convince the girls that we should mingle with some of the other patrons to see who we could meet.

That was the only thought in my mind as I gave myself one last look over before walking over to the bathroom door and opening it.

That was until I saw him.

15

RAVEN

I stood there frozen in place as I studied him. Any buzz that I had from the alcohol was gone, and I got the opportunity to take him in. I would never admit this out loud, but I was questioning how it was possible to be both turned on by him but also afraid of what he might do to me. His blond hair looked as if he'd been tugging on it, and his white dress shirt was unbuttoned at the neck and looked slightly wrinkled. Seeing him somewhat undone made me wonder what he'd been doing before he'd found me.

No matter how good he looked, I was irritated that he was here. "You've got to be kidding me."

"There's no kidding here, little bird."

I hadn't heard that nickname in years and it sent a tremble through my body. Or maybe it was the look in Nash's eye when he said it. It was obvious who was the hunter and who was the prey. He took a step forward and I wondered if he was going to push me back through the bathroom door. Instead, he grabbed my arm and dragged me farther down the dark hallway as I fought against him. I tried to scream, but it was no use. The music was playing too loud, drowning out any chance of me being heard.

He finally stopped and backed me into the wall. There were barely a few inches between us as he crowded me. To anyone who might see us, it might look like a couple having an intimate moment, but I knew better. The intense stare in his eyes wasn't because of lust, it was because of anger.

I knew it was because of the text message I'd sent. I hadn't expected to see him so soon after I sent it.

"You're leaving with me right now."

His voice was low and dangerous, but I refused to be intimidated. "No. I'm not, and you can kiss my—"

My words were cut off as he bent down, and before I knew it, I was getting an eyeful of his ass because he'd thrown me over his shoulder.

"Let me down, you asshole!" I screamed as I beat on his back. I used every ounce of my strength to make sure he knew how pissed I was that this was happening, but it didn't matter. His grip on me tightened and a loud creak that met a swift gust of wind told me that we were outside. If anyone was near us, they were, for sure, getting an eyeful of my ass. I screamed again, but all of that was temporary because the next thing I knew, I was being thrown into the passenger seat of a fancy sports car.

"What you're going to do now is be quiet this entire drive unless I speak to you. Got it?"

"And if I'm not?"

"You don't want to add to the punishment you're going to get for beating on my back."

"But you were—"

I stopped speaking because he'd shut the door and I

watched as he was walking around the car to the driver's side. It seemed as if he'd taken me out the back entrance of Elevate, probably to avoid making a scene. I was stunned that no one had seen him take me out of the club. Or maybe people had and they didn't give a damn.

I scrambled to get my purse open so I could either call 9-1-1 or Izzy. 9-1-1 was probably the better bet since who knew what state Izzy was in and if she might be able to answer her phone. When Nash opened the driver's door, I was about to press send when he snatched the phone out of my hand and sat in the driver's seat. Before I could yell at him, he gave me a pointed glare, daring me to make a sound after what he'd just said.

Nash pocketed my phone and locked the car doors. I knew I had no other recourse outside of putting my seat belt on and going along for the drive, because if I ran, there was no doubt in my mind that he would catch me, given my current state.

He turned the engine on, and I listened to the car come to life. I knew little about sports cars but by the way this one looked and sounded, I knew it must have cost a hefty penny.

Nash guided the car out of the alleyway and turned onto the street. We were driving into the night, and I had no idea where it would take me.

NASH ENDED up taking me to a luxury apartment that wasn't too far from Elevate. I only knew that because I spent the entire car ride watching the clock on the dashboard and we drove for less than fifteen minutes. When he parked the car in an underground garage, I waited as he stepped around to open the passenger door for me. We still hadn't said a word to one another as we left the car, rode up in an elevator, and walked into what I assume was his parents' place.

While he shut the door, I quickly took in the space we were in. It differed from his apartment in Brentson. This apartment was designed with a more traditional feel and had more neutral colors, like my apartment. It, too, had all the latest appliances and gadgets, and given our location, I knew it had to have cost a fortune.

Nash grabbed some mail and looked through it. I knew he probably didn't give a damn about it and was doing it to make me more anxious.

I cleared my throat and said, "Give me my phone."

"You'll get it back when I say you do."

"Give it back to me."

The look on Nash's face dared me to continue. His facial expression was downright frightening, and it brought back memories of my encounter with him in the library. My filter couldn't catch my words in time, and I asked, "Are you going to kill me?"

Nash stared at me like I had grown another head. Then a smile appeared on his lips. "Do you want me to?"

"It might be a hell of a lot better than whatever you have planned for me if you had to resort to kidnapping me in order to do it."

"I didn't kidnap you."

That did it. His nonchalant response set me off.

"You are the biggest piece of—"

He had no problem cutting me off. "Please tell me why I'm a piece of shit, Goodwin."

"Because you set me up. There was no way I was going to get to your apartment within the hour if I was here. And you knew where I was because you had no problem showing up and dragging me out of there."

"I didn't drag you anywhere."

"Okay, since you want to get technical, you picked me up and threw me into your car. Does that work?"

"Sure, if that helps you feel better."

But he didn't deny the rest of what I said. "You set this all up. Admit it."

He shrugged. "I did."

There was no remorse in his words. Instead, his response felt like a dare. Daring me to say anything else.

"Just start your fucking game."

"Patience would look better on you."

His words further irritated me to the point I wanted to throw something at him. Deep down, I knew it wasn't smart and that he more than likely could dodge anything I threw because of his athletic ability, but it didn't mean I didn't want to try.

Nash walked toward me, and my body immediately stiffened. When he didn't approach me like expected, I was left staring at him, wondering what he was going to do next. He strolled over to the couch like he had no care in the world and sat down.

Once he was settled, he pulled his phone out and looked to be scrolling. I couldn't see what though from where I was standing. This must have been his way of teaching me a lesson about being patient.

I wasn't sure how long I stood there before he finally looked over and acknowledged me.

"Come here."

I hated how those two words made my heart skip a beat. If he was determined to keep me off balance, he was doing an excellent job. I glanced at the door, wishing that someone would come through and stop whatever madness he had planned. Would it be worth it to try to open the door and run for help?

"Don't even think about it," he said.

I hated that he could read my thoughts. Now that he knew what I was thinking about, the opportunity behind that door had closed.

"I want you to strip."

I hid my shock by not making a move as his words caused my skin to flush. *How dare he?*

It was because he was Nash Henson, and he could crush everything I worked so hard for with the flick of his hand.

"I know you can do better than that. Remove the dress. Slowly."

I froze. My goal had been to come here and reason with him. He'd always been so easy to talk to and there was no way that had changed in the two years I'd been gone. It was clear I was wrong.

Bile rose in my throat as I thought about him carrying this out. Deep down, I'd hoped he would let all of this go and it wasn't until now that I truly feared the ramifications of his sick, twisted game.

My dress left little to the imagination to begin with. When I made a move to grab the fabric, Nash made a tsking sound and I stopped moving.

"Slide the straps down your arms, and then pull it down. I want to see your tits bouncing."

I thought humiliation would have pierced my consciousness and I could feel my skin heating at his words. But there was something else there too. "You know, I never would've thought that you would've turned out to be such an asshole."

"Feeling's mutual, sweetheart." Sarcasm was laced through his words as his eyes watched me pull one of my straps down my arm. "You know what I regret?"

I refuse to dignify him with an answer, but that didn't stop him from continuing.

"I regret not getting my complete fill of this pussy before you fled town. That all changes now."

It hurt that he referred to the time we spent together as such. I didn't expect to feel that way about it, and that realization hurt more than the demeaning act he had me doing right now. Slowly, I slid the other strap down my arm. I pushed the rest of the fabric down my body and stepped out of it, leaving me in just the lacy thong I wore tonight and the high-heeled boots I'd paired with Izzy's dress.

Nash shifted in his seat as his eyes burned a hole into me, crushing feelings I'd thought I had buried long ago. Those emotions were unleashed and were more complicated than ever. Deep down, I knew that the boy I'd fallen in love with was still there, hiding behind this facade he'd put up to keep anyone from getting too close.

I pushed my shoulders back as the reason I left Brentson in the first place flashed in my mind. His eyes took their time perusing the sight before him. "Still as fucking hot as ever."

His words had always been something I loved about him. He could turn me on just by saying something in a certain way, let alone when he was actually saying dirty words. Over the time I'd been away, I chalked it up to me not having much experience with other men, but it was clear even though we couldn't stand one another, he still had this power over me.

This was it. This was what I was doing to make sure Nash didn't leak my secret.

"Come here." I barely understood what he said because of how low his voice had become.

I strolled over to him, suddenly unsure of my steps. The confidence I'd had earlier in the night when I left our hotel was gone, but any signs of humiliation that I thought would take its place weren't there. Nash couldn't take his eyes off of me and was obviously affected by the sight in front of him. By the way he pulled at his pants and readjusted himself, I could see he was having a hard time keeping it together.

A sense of pride grew in the pit of my stomach. While in his mind he might hate me, his body had other plans.

"Sit down on my lap, your back against my chest."

That hadn't been what I was expecting him to say. Rather than spend more time questioning it, I did as I was told. How he was affected by my almost naked body was undeniable now as I felt his cock underneath my bare ass. But my attention didn't remain there for long.

His hand traced an imaginary line up and down my arm before reaching around to grab my breasts. I didn't want to give in to his touch, but it was as if I had no choice. My body had a mind of its own and all signs were pointed at the pleasure that was building in the pit of my stomach. Nash teased my nipples until they were stiff peaks. I hoped he would turn me around and suck on them, but I refused to voice that need out loud.

When his hand left my breast, I sighed in annoyance, but that feeling was soon erased as I watched where he was going. I could feel his breath tickling my ear as his hand traveled down my body until he reached my pussy. Nash used one of his hands to rub up and down my panty-covered lips as I squirmed under his touch.

Fuck me, Nash. Fuck me.

Thankfully, I'd only said that mantra in my head, although it would become evident how desperate I was for him to fuck me. As if he'd heard my thoughts once again, he moved my panties to the side and found my clit. When he touched it for the first time, my back arched, and I heard a growl leave his lips.

Nash took his time playing with my clit, using his finger to dance along my slit and back to my clit before doing it all over again. It was as if he were playing a game designed only for him. I could feel my arousal and I wouldn't be surprised if I'd left remnants of the effect he was having on me on his pants.

He used his other arm to wrap around my lower half, anchoring me against his body and used that hand's fingers to keep my thong out of the way.

The fingers that were playing with my clit came to a stop and I gasped when they finally gave me what I wanted and slid his finger inside of me.

Our connection and the low moans from me were the only sounds that could be heard in the room. It should embarrass me that he could turn me into this, but I didn't care. Nothing else mattered. All I wanted was for him to help me reach my climax.

My breath became more labored, and I could feel that I was closing in on the edge. He must have noticed it too, because his movements slowed and he pulled his finger away, deciding instead to run his fingers up and down my lips again. Just as my frustration grew, he slid his finger inside of me and went back to fucking me again. I imagined it was his cock, and as I came closer to going over the edge again, he stopped.

"Fuck you!" I sounded desperate and didn't care.

"Do you want to come?" I heard the smile in his voice.

I nodded eagerly as my fingers clenched his thighs. If he hadn't been wearing a pair of black slacks, I knew I would have left marks on them with my fingernails. Deep down, I knew he was going to bring me to the brink of an orgasm again, and then snatch it away. It was another way for him to torture me and to show how much power he had over me. When he did it again, I screamed in frustration.

"That's what I wanted to hear," he whispered in my ear. His finger slid inside of me and fucked me with a vigor that hadn't been found when he was teasing me before. It was as if every time before this was an appetizer and now we were starting the main course.

I moaned loudly as I rode his hand, determined that this time would be it. This time, I would get what I wanted.

My body finally careened out of control as the pleasure that had been building up over the course of his teasing was finally let loose, free from the hold he had on me. I leaned back onto his shoulder and closed my eyes. If you would have told me that I would be lying in Nash's arms right now, I would have called you a liar.

"I could stick my cock in this beautiful pussy right now and you'd be nothing but welcoming."

His words permeated the euphoria I was in, and I hated that he was right.

"But I'm not going to."

It irritated me that I felt disappointed by his words as his finger continued to slide up and down my slit, coating more of my pussy in my arousal.

"When I fuck you, I want you to remember every single second, angle, position, and sound that we make together."

I shivered involuntarily. Nash grasped my body again before picking me up and placing me on the cushion beside him. "You need to clean up and get dressed. I'll get you a washcloth."

His words were like a jug of ice water poured all over my body. It was as if I'd been awakened from a deep sleep. I fixed my underwear and scrambled to get up off the couch and walked over to the dress I'd left on the floor. I picked it up and held it against my chest, which seemed foolish given what we'd just done.

"Just tell me where the bathroom is, and I'll be done and out of here in five minutes."

Nash looked at me weirdly before pointing to a door. I almost ran away from him but thought better of it. Instead, I walked into the bathroom like normal and closed the door behind me a little harder than necessary. It was then I took a deep breath and came to terms with what I'd done.

16

RAVEN

The rest of my time in NYC passed by in a blur. It was either due to how much of a whirlwind Friday was or it was because of what Nash and I had done.

Deep down, I knew it was the latter even though I tried to convince myself it was because of the former. I returned the text messages that I'd received while I was with Nash and told the girls I would meet them back at the hotel when they returned. Although they offered to meet up with me, I didn't feel like going back out to continue my night on the town. It wasn't my scene anyway, and I wasn't about to turn down a relaxing evening in a hotel room. I kept my phone's ringtone on in case anyone needed me to go to them, but other than that, I was planning on vegging out and taking a nap.

But even after all of my relaxation attempts, my brain wouldn't shut off.

I finally dozed off, and the girls came back to the hotel room around two in the morning, and I immediately got to work trying to help take care of Izzy, who was by far the worst off. If she swore off drinking for a while, I wouldn't be surprised, but what a way to bring in your twenty-first birthday.

None of the girls had bothered to ask me about where I was, so I assumed my texts had done a thorough job of convincing them that I was okay. I knew that if Izzy had been in the right frame of mind, she would have caused a bigger ruckus, but I assumed Lila and Erika thought I'd probably gone and hooked up with someone. And they wouldn't be wrong.

Lila offered to drive Izzy's car back to Brentson on Saturday because she was in no shape to. While I would have hoped we could have spent more time in the city, homework and other obligations were calling and we decided that we probably needed the rest of Saturday and all of Sunday to catch up. I offered to sit in the back seat with Izzy in case things with her took a turn for the worse, and I figured that was the least I could do because Lila and Erika had taken care of her after Nash snatched me from the club.

Izzy slept for most of the ride back to Brentson, leaving me to my thoughts about Nash. I hadn't heard from him since Friday night, and I didn't know if deep down I'd been expecting to. I refused to dwell on what happened because there was nothing I could do to change it.

And I didn't want to.

That was a bitter pill to swallow. I couldn't stand him, but I liked the way he made me feel. I liked the effect I had on him, and would I do it again? Maybe.

The chances of it happening again were high if this was all that his game was meant to be. I was allowed to find some enjoyment out of it if I could. Now would I ever admit that out loud? Debatable.

The entire car ride back to campus was quiet. The four of us tossed our bags inside of our apartment and went into our respective rooms to take naps and try to recover from the adventure we'd had on Friday night.

When I woke up ninety minutes later, my stomach growled as I was pulling myself out of bed. The urge to have fast food delivered to the apartment was strong, but I refrained, instead choosing to grab a couple of frozen pizzas that we'd stored in the freezer for emergencies like this. As I was sticking the pizza in the oven, I heard a door open. Someone else must have woken up around the same time I had.

After I closed the oven door, I turned and found Izzy walking into the kitchen. Her hair was a mess and not even the makeshift ponytail she'd thrown it into would help.

"Good morning, sunshine," I said sarcastically. "Can I get you a cup of coffee? Caffeine will help."

Izzy sat down at the dining room table, placed the bottle of water she'd been carrying in front of her and closed her eyes. "Yeah, that would be great, and a glass of water, if you don't mind."

I made her a cup of coffee and placed it next to the water.

"Where did you go while we were all still at Elevate?"

Izzy knew how to cut right to the chase. No "hellos," or "how are yous." Even in her hungover state she was determined to get the answers she desired. I debated lying and making her think I was there the whole time, but that was a pretty fucked up thing to do. Plus, I'd abandoned her on her special day, so the least I could do was be truthful.

"Nash showed up."

My announcement made her sit up quickly, and I could

see that she immediately regretted it. She winced, and I pointed at the bottle of water. She took a sip before she continued. "That would then make sense as to why Easton was there."

"Easton?"

Izzy took a deep breath and let it out. Hopefully, that would provide some relief for what I assumed was her spinning head. "Nash's best friend. He showed up at Elevate after you took off. I remember getting pissed at him because he said he knew where you were and that we had to trust that you were safe with him. I asked him to prove it and we got into it, but honestly, things got so hazy that I didn't follow up on it. That's so fucked up."

"Don't beat yourself up about it. I'm fine."

"But what if you hadn't been?"

"Let's not think about it now but put precautions into place in case something like this were to ever happen again."

That seemed to placate Izzy, and she took a sip of the hot coffee in front of her. I was still stuck on what she said. Easton hadn't been his best friend when we were dating, but it was obvious that he was complicit in the stunt that Nash pulled. How much did he know about this? Would it be worth approaching him to see if I could find out what the hell this was all about?

The plan that was coming together in my head was a nice thought at first, but Easton's loyalty would lie with Nash. Easton wouldn't tell me anything.

"So, what happened with Nash?"

Izzy's words cut through the noise in my mind and I couldn't look at her. There was no way I could tell her the truth about the game Nash was blackmailing me into that had brought me undeniable pleasure just the night before.

"Nash wanted to talk. About the incident at the library. Said he felt guilty about what he'd done."

Izzy looked at me skeptically, but what I said must have been enough. "And how did that go?"

"Good, I think. We've reached an understanding and he won't do that again."

"Did you talk about why you left Brentson our senior year?"

I shook my head. "No, we didn't get around to it."

"Strange. When I handed him the note you left, he seemed to have a lot of questions that went along with the anger he was feeling. If you guys spoke, he had the opportunity to ask you about, well, everything, and didn't. That's weird."

"Yeah, I'm not sure why he didn't."

I didn't tell her it was because he thought he had all the answers. I didn't tell her it was because he knew of what I'd done to his father. What I did know was that he had no intention of learning the truth because it didn't fit into his narrative of me being the biggest bitch on the planet, and he had no problem hate fucking me to get his revenge.

17

NASH

The thrill of winning a football game would never get old. I couldn't help but grin as I high fived my teammates. Plans were being made about whose house we would party at when we got back to campus. Today's game was an away game, and I couldn't wait to be on the bus back to Brentson.

When we finally hit the road, I put my earbuds in and drowned out the noise that was coming from my teammates and our coaches. Everyone knew by now that I usually took the time while we traveled to either get my mind into the game or to decompress from the game we'd just had. I liked to run through things I did well and what I could have done better.

After I went over several plays from the game, I found my thoughts drifting from today's game to Raven. The last time I saw her was last weekend when I brought her back to my parents' apartment in the city. I used it from time to time, especially when I interned in New York City during the summers after my freshmen and sophomore years. Dad and

Mom would stay there when they had functions in the city and sometimes had friends stay if they were visiting and the apartment wasn't in use. It came in handy to have access to the place, especially last Friday.

I spent most of my time replaying Raven coming all over my fingers again. And again. I wanted her again. I craved seeing her fall apart in my arms again to the point where a lot of my thoughts drifted back to her. Working her out of my system seemed to be the only option and I hazard a guess that was why her name was written on the envelope that was handed to me after my first test in front of the Chevalier leadership.

They'd known she was my weakness. I wasn't sure how they'd found out, but they knew. And now this was my test.

I fiddled with my phone as I debated sending her a text. I'd probably be back in Brentson in an hour and a half or two hours, max. It would be nice to get rid of this extra adrenaline I was feeling after the game. One would think that I would be tired after the physical exertion I'd just endured, but the thought of having her provided a sense of excitement that the football game couldn't bring. I double-checked that I had nothing else going on tonight and decided I would stop by the celebration party, but after that, I had other plans for tonight.

Me: ***Be ready for me to pick you up at 10 p.m.***

Someone pulled my right earbud out of my ear. He was lucky he spoke before I said something I'd regret.

"Which parties are you hitting up tonight?" Easton got comfortable in the seat beside me as if I invited him to sit there.

I snatched the earphone back from him before I replied, "I think I'm just going to hit up the one at the football house."

Easton blinked once, and then twice. "That can't be the only party you plan on attending. We just won a major game."

"I know that. I was there, making plays on the field."

Easton raised an eyebrow at me and leaned in closer to make sure I was the only one that could hear what he was going to say. "What's gotten into you? All last year we were partying it up and now, it seems to be the last thing you want to do... outside of traveling to New York City on a whim, and then disappearing for a couple of hours. You still owe me for distracting Izzy, Erika, and Lila, you know."

"Maybe I'm all partied out."

"Or you were trying to fuck their other roommate. What's her name? People were talking shit about her—"

That caught my attention. I grabbed Easton's arm and held on tight. "Who was talking about her and what were they saying?"

"Ouch, dude, fuck."

I loosened my grip on his arm before letting go. Hurting him hadn't been my intention, but it had been instinctual. "What did you hear?"

"I wasn't here when whatever shit went down with her happened, but people were just saying they couldn't believe she was back after what had happened to her mother."

I was surprised that was the reason people were talking. Yes, her mother's death was tragic but there had been rumors flying around about us when she left that had really set the gossip mill turning.

"You were mentioned a bit too."

Ah, there it is.

"Fascinating. And what did they say about her and me?"

"That she had some nerve showing her face back here after she disappeared the day after you both graduated from high school."

That was accurate and I still didn't know why she was here. It hadn't been something that came up while I was fucking her with my finger on my parents' couch.

"So I'll rephrase my question. Is the reason why you're missing out on all of the parties that are sure to happen tonight because of her?"

My phone chose right then to vibrate in my hand, but I didn't bother looking at the screen because I knew who it was. And I didn't need Easton knowing more than he already did.

"Maybe. Got to get my dick wet some kind of way."

Easton almost choked. "Since when have you ever had a problem getting pussy?"

That was true. I'd never had a problem finding a girl to fuck, but Raven had me in a chokehold that I needed to get loose from. If it took skipping a bunch of parties temporarily to do so, then so be it.

"She has you fucked up."

I glared at Easton out of the corner of my eye but didn't confirm or deny his claim.

"How long have we known each other for, Nash?"

"Since freshman year."

"And I've never seen you this worked up over a girl."

"I'm not worked up over her."

Easton chuckled. "If that's what helps you to sleep more peacefully at night, so be it."

I *wasn't* worked up over her. The only thing feeding my desire to have her was revenge. I rolled my eyes at Easton and put my earbud back in, determined to ignore the rest of the world once more. I turned my attention to the scenery out of my window and waited a few minutes until I was confident enough that Easton had gotten bored and was paying attention to something else. When I spotted Easton talking to someone out of the corner of my eye, I dared to look at my phone. Just as I suspected, a text from Raven was waiting for me to read.

Raven: ***The least you can do is ask.***

Me: ***Why should I ask when I already know what you're going to do?***

I smirked as I saw that she was typing back. Sparring with her now would make this evening a lot sweeter.

Raven: ***Are we ever going to talk about what happened? I would like to explain my side of the story.***

I stared at her message for longer than necessary. While I should always expect the unexpected, I was taken by surprise by the current message. Talking about what happened would only further screw up this situation. Maybe I'd feel differently in the future, but for now, I had no intention of talking about that day.

Me: ***No, we aren't. 10 p.m.***

I put my phone away and vowed not to talk to Raven again until I saw her later this evening. I allowed the music to take me away for the duration of the journey back to Brentson.

As I was stepping off the team bus, I looked up and found Landon standing there. *What the fuck is he doing here?*

Before I could walk over to him, a slap on my shoulder

drew my attention to Easton, who was looking at me with a big grin. "You are going to at least go to the football party tonight, right?"

"Yes, I already told you that."

"Just making sure. Didn't want you backing out."

I shook my head at him and looked at where I'd last seen Landon.

But he was gone.

18

NASH

I sat outside her house in my sports car about ten minutes before ten. To look even more pathetic, I'd left the party I attended with Easton fifteen minutes earlier than I needed to and drove around her block several times to waste even more time.

Now I scrolled through my phone, skimming through jewelry listings as I waited for the clock to approach the time I'd set for Raven to meet me outside. When I spontaneously clicked the buy button on the item my attention had been drawn to, I had no regrets.

By now, I should have been tired, but the anticipation of what this night would bring wiped any sense of tiredness from my body. A moment that had been years in the making was upon me, whether Raven knew it or not. I was parked in front of her apartment, blocking her car and another in the driveway. It wasn't like she would need it anyway.

I remembered walking up to her house while we were dating in high school and knocking on her door. I would talk with her mom while I waited for her to come downstairs so that we could go on our dates. Walking her from her door to my car and opening the car door was one of the ways in which my parents had forced me to have proper manners. While the instinct to perform those actions was still there, I refused to make more of this than what it already was. This whole arrangement was payback and just a way for me to get her out of my system as quickly as possible. It was important that I didn't give her the idea that this was something more.

I happened to look out of my side-view mirror and saw an SUV slowly approaching. I wouldn't have thought anything of it if the car's headlights weren't turned low. If the driver was looking for something, they would have made their attempt harder by not having their headlights on.

Everything in me screamed out about how sketchy this was. It reminded me of what I saw when I stopped by her house after the library incident. What the driver of the vehicle didn't know was that I was also here, ready and willing to confront this motherfucker.

When the SUV got closer to my car, I threw open my car door, forcing the driver to break. I climbed out of the car and tried to rush to the driver's side of the other vehicle, but whoever it was caught onto what I was trying to do.

They turned their high beams on and threw the car in reverse. Whoever it was, they were lucky that there was no one else coming down the street to stop them. I chased after them, but quickly realized it was no use because I was no match for a moving vehicle. All of this happened in a matter of seconds and while I caught a glimpse of the driver, it wasn't enough to give me much information on their appearance.

"You son of a—" I stopped the words from leaving my mouth because it wouldn't help this situation.

"Nash?"

I turned to find Raven standing on the sidewalk in front of her house. Between all the distractions, I hadn't heard her open the door and step outside.

"Get in the car, Goodwin."

She rolled her eyes but opened the passenger side door. I followed suit and soon we were driving down the street.

Our car ride was silent at first and I was surprised she didn't have more to say about my texting her last minute again. I ended the silence because the incident we'd just left was irritating me. "Have you noticed anyone watching your home?"

My question clearly took her by surprise because out of the corner of my eye, I saw her snap her head in my direction before she spoke. "What does that matter to you?"

Raven was right. Why did I care? I couldn't give her that answer because I didn't know why myself, so I deflected. "Answer the damn question."

She sighed and said, "No? Should I have noticed something?"

I wondered how much I should tell her because letting her in on everything I knew would give away that I had come to her place after our "meeting" at the library.

"While I was waiting for you, I saw an SUV slowly driving down your street. When the driver noticed me here, they threw it in reverse and backed away." I didn't turn to look at her while I explained a version of events that wasn't completely true.

"That isn't really all that strange though..." Her voice

trailed off, and I wondered if she was waiting for me to expound on my reasoning.

"It wouldn't have been for me either if the driver hadn't thrown the car in reverse. Looked like whoever was driving was trying to get away as quickly as possible."

I took a chance and glanced at her out of the corner of my eye before turning my attention back to the road. She was slowly nodding her head, and I could tell she was buying what I was saying.

"I guess that is a little odd now that you mention it. But no, I haven't noticed anybody waiting outside my apartment or anything like that. I'll be sure to pay attention from now on. Where are we going?"

The swift change in the subject startled me, but I quickly regained my footing. "Back to my place."

"I should have known that," Raven mumbled. Her words were just above a whisper, and I wasn't sure if she wanted me to hear them. I didn't bother responding but I spared another glance at her. She'd turned her attention to staring out the window, choosing to focus on the outside scenery instead of the mounting tension in the car.

Her question from moments ago was still at the forefront of my mind. *Why did I care?* That would take more time to dissect than I was prepared to spend at the moment. Despite that, it was still a valid question.

Even when I tried to push the thoughts aside, I still found myself looking for an explanation for all of this that went beyond the need to get revenge. Because revenge did not mean scrolling through a famous jewelry store's website and dropping thousands without second-guessing it. There was this need to own her in every way possible, and I assumed the piece of jewelry I'd bought for her was an extension of that.

Yes, that would explain why I just spent a lot of money on the gift I'd brought her. Maybe I should consider it a present she could pawn off that would help wipe her tears when I was done with her.

19

RAVEN

"How'd the game go?"

"Since when are you interested in my football games?"

I rolled my eyes. "I was always invested in how well you were doing in different avenues of your life, including football, because of how much you loved it..."

"You used to be invested."

Of course, he had to go there. I'd been back in Brentson for weeks now and he was still alluding to my two years away. Then again, maybe it was fair game since he hadn't gotten two years' worth of verbal hits in yet.

What he didn't know was that I beat myself up enough for the both of us over the last two years. I wanted to come back multiple times, but I didn't because I was afraid, and I didn't have anything motivating me to come back. The only people who were here that I cared about were Izzy, who visited me occasionally, and Nash, who I figured had moved on anyway. But clearly, he hadn't.

Nash and I arrived back at his place in a different fashion

than when I had come here previously. Instead of dread filling me, I knew what was coming and had done enough to prepare myself. I hoped.

After Nash opened the door to his apartment, he tossed his keys on the small table near the door, and in a flash, he was on me. He backed me into his front door, took his thumb and ran it across my lips, smearing the tinted lip gloss I'd put on just before stepping outside to meet him.

His touch left my face ablaze. My cheeks grew warmer the longer he stared at me. The look on his face turned animalistic as he followed the trail that my lip gloss left behind. That only lasted a moment because then his lips were on mine.

His hands held my cheeks, anchoring my lips to his. The kiss was anything but sweet. Gone were the memories of how softly he used to kiss me and in their place was the wicked nature that he'd adopted. It was as if seeing me like this flipped a switch within him because nothing about the ride over here gave me any indication that this was how things would go.

It took me a second to catch up with his intensity, but when I did, he groaned against my lips. The sound further enticed me, and I grabbed a hold of his shirt to bring him closer to me.

Our kissing continued as our tongues battled it out to see who would be the victor. I felt his fingertips leave my face and travel down to my black hoodie. He grasped my breasts and growled. He broke our kiss and took a step back before he yanked the clothing over my head.

"You waste no time, huh?"

"I've been thinking about this moment all day. It feels like I've been waiting forever."

Nash took this as an opportunity to take off my T-shirt too. I'd made sure to put on a matching black lacy bra and thong before coming here because of the confidence it gave me. It seemed as if he enjoyed the last time I wore lace around him too.

He studied me, committing every curve to memory, and then he said, "There's no use in lying. We both know how much you wanted this, dating back to when we were in high school. The couple of times we'd fucked weren't enough and you know it."

His words sent a shiver down my spine. "I should have never given you the time of day back in high school."

He couldn't hide his reaction to my words behind the facade he'd built. The way that his head snapped in my direction, the narrowing of his eyes, his lips pressed together. "I see that you're continuing to lie to yourself. Forming bad habits isn't a good thing."

"Listen—"

"While arguing with you is a turn on, the only thing I want to hear coming from your fucking lips are your moans or chanting my name repeatedly."

His tone was mocking, but the look in his eyes wasn't. His words did their job because whatever I was thinking of saying was long gone.

Nash leaned forward and kissed me again, with the same vigor as before. This time, the sweatshirt didn't hinder his ability to grab my breasts through my bra. His lips left mine and trailed kisses down my neck and to my chest. While I thought he was going to focus his attention on my breasts, he instead left a sensual kiss on each breast before kissing his way down my body.

He ended up on his knees in front of me, kissing me just above the waistband of my jeans. Nash slowly unbuttoned and unzipped my jeans and pushed them down my legs, allowing me to step out of them.

He looked as if he was debating attacking me from where he kneeled before me, but he quickly stood up and picked me up. I squealed from the shock and soon he sat me on the island. When I was expecting my bare ass to hit the counter, it didn't because he'd laid a bath towel on it. Someone had been preparing for this.

I watched as he walked over to a bottle of champagne that was chilling in a fancy silver ice bucket.

"Figured you were more of a beer kind of guy."

"There's a lot you don't know about me, Goodwin. Now take the bra off and lay down on the counter. Things might get messy."

The fluttering in my stomach told me that I wanted things to get messy in more ways than he might have been referring to. I did as he requested and laid on my back. My hand grazed the lace of my panties, reminding me that I hadn't removed my underwear.

"What about—"

"What did I say?"

His voice shut me up. Just when I started to feel awkward, I heard the cork pop, and I jumped at the sudden sound in the quiet room. He walked over to me and dragged a finger down my torso. I was this close to begging him to do more, but his warning from earlier was still at the forefront of my mind, and he spoke first.

"My own buffet. Who would have thought?"

I'd expected his words to be filled with sarcasm, but I

found lust. I turned my head so I could watch him while he took a swig from the bottle of champagne before he poured a tiny bit in between my breasts. The chill from the liquid made goosebumps appear on my skin, but the coolness was short-lived. His mouth quickly followed, and he licked up every last drop. But that wasn't where this adventure ended. He smirked at me before his tour of my body continued to my breast. He allowed some of the liquid to fall onto my nipple before his mouth joined the party, bringing my nipple to a stiff peak.

When I moaned, I heard him chuckle against my breast.

"That's not funny."

Nash hit my breast, not enough to hurt me, but enough to shock me into silence. He kissed the spot he hit.

"Hmm... you liked that, didn't you?" He didn't wait for me to answer his question. "Good to know."

He took his time licking the champagne off my breasts before placing the champagne near my head. "Have some. I'm about to be drinking something else."

I leaned on my elbows and grabbed the champagne bottle while he took his T-shirt off and walked to the other end of the counter. He undressed completely while I drank from the bottle, and then he pulled my legs forward. When he bent down, he had direct access to my pussy. I took one last sip from the bottle as he ran two fingers along my pussy lips. Knowing there was no way I was going to hold the bottle without the potential of having it shatter on the counter or the floor, I put it arm's length away, hoping to avoid an accident. I watched as he removed my panties and his eyes met mine from his place between my legs. His stare shook me to my core.

Nash leaned forward and licked my pussy. My head immediately fell back and I sighed, content with him touching my body. Another moan left my lips. Part of me was irritated that I was giving him what he wanted, but he was also giving me what I wanted. What I needed.

I couldn't keep track of anything while his mouth was on me. I could feel him alternating between licking and sucking. The pressure within me was building, and the smirk on his face told me he knew what he was doing to me. But then he stopped. He stood up to his full height with the smirk still firmly in place.

"You only come when I'm ready for you to come."

He used his fingers to run up and down my lips again, taking his time and watching me squirm.

"If you don't—"

"If I don't what, Goodwin?"

Him saying my last name in the way that shouted out how much he despised me was like getting sprinkled with cold water. Not enough to take me out of the moment we were having, but it was a wake-up call.

Then he stuck a finger inside of me, distracting me from what had just occurred. "You're so tight... fuck."

"Oh my—"

Another surge of pleasure filled my body as I groaned out loud. I moved so that I could sit up, and while it took longer than usual because of him fingering me, it was well worth it. I got to look into the blue eyes that I used to know so well, now darkened by desire. The desire to kiss him again was there, but I refrained because it might slow him down.

When he added another finger to my pussy, the intensity began to build within me again. I groaned, worried he might stop his motions. I was half expecting him to stop since that had become a part of the game we played. When he didn't and I could feel myself getting closer to my climax, I could have cried. I ground into his hand, unashamed at what he was causing my body to do.

"I want you to come for me, and then I'm going to fuck this tight pussy."

That set off a chain reaction. I screamed his name out loud as I came hard. He took his fingers out of me and licked each one.

"Get off the island and turn around so that your ass faces me. And spread your legs."

I did as he said and looked over at Nash. He was busy unwrapping a condom. I turned around and the hairs on my body were standing at attention. Nash stepped up behind me and pulled on my ponytail. He whispered in my ear, "Once I stick my cock in, that's it. You're fucking mine until I say that you're not. Do you know what else is going to happen?"

I shook my head quickly in an effort to lessen the time it would take for him to put me out of my misery.

"I'm going to fuck you so hard that everyone in this building will know my damn name."

He pushed me forward so that I was leaning on the countertop, forcing my ass to stick out a bit. Nash ran his cock along my pussy before entering me. There was no teasing with him when it came to this. He pulled all the way out before sticking his cock into me so fast that I cried out. This felt so damn good, and I wondered how I'd gone for two years without this.

Because you left without a trace, Raven.

But someone knew where I was because they'd dragged me back here.

Any thoughts of anyone else were quickly gone when Nash thrust into me again, setting a pace I wasn't sure my body could keep up with. But quickly enough, my body naturally began meeting every one of his thrusts.

"Nash. Oh my—Nash." He was right again. His name became a mantra, but this time he didn't chuckle or try to mock me. I was convinced he was too busy trying to fuck me to death.

"Fuck..." Nash's words trailed off, and I wondered if he said the word involuntarily.

"I'm going to come again."

"Good," Nash ground out. His hand came around to my front and found my clit. And that was all the encouragement my body needed.

My orgasm came in hard and sent me into a euphoric state that I'd never experienced before. Nash mumbled behind me and thrust into me until he joined me in orgasmic bliss.

We were both left breathing hard, and I used the countertop to support my weight because I didn't trust that my legs could keep me upright. If hate fucking felt this amazing, he could hate me for the rest of our lives.

20

RAVEN

"Raven?" Izzy's voice carried from the front door and into the living room.

I looked up from the television show I was watching. I'd just finished my homework and was relaxing on the couch. Today had gone better and I was able to concentrate more easily than normal. "Yeah?"

"You have mail."

A quick glance at my phone proved to me that it was seven in the evening. Had the mail person really come this late? I stood up and stretched. When I started for the door, I said, "That's strange. I thought the mail was delivered earlier today."

"I'm not sure. This is the first time I've been home since this morning."

She handed an envelope to me and just stared at the front of it. All it had on it was my name. No return address or stamp. It hadn't been delivered through the mail, which meant someone had dropped it on my doorstep.

Every hair on my body stood at attention. It almost

mirrored the letter that was in my room that brought me here.

I ripped open the envelope too quickly. Izzy probably thought something was wrong with me, but I didn't care.

Be careful who you're involved with. You don't want to end up like your mother.

I immediately knew who it was, recognized the handwriting. This letter was shorter than the one I'd received, urging me to go to Brentson, but was still from the same sender.

"What's wrong?"

I tried my best to pull my expression back to normal. I sucked the few times I played poker, so I knew it was more than likely going to be a fail on my part.

Izzy took a step toward me and placed a hand on my shoulder. "What happened?"

I handed her the piece of paper and walked away. My feet took me into my bedroom, and I soon found myself pulling at one of the suitcases in my closet. I could hear Izzy's footsteps quickly joining me in my room, but she said nothing as I yanked the bag out and tossed it onto my neatly made bed.

It was easy for me to find the letter because it was the only thing still in the suitcase. I handed the letter to Izzy so that she, too, could read it.

R.,

The time has come. If you want to know what happened to your mother, you will come back to Brentson. You will receive further instructions soon.

That letter was also unsigned.

When Izzy said nothing after reading the letter out loud, I said, "I assumed that the instructions coming soon were regarding the acceptance letter I received a day later from Brentson. This letter has to be from the same person."

"Or people."

Izzy's suggestion that it might be more than one person never occurred to me. It would make more sense since both letters were delivered in person versus through the mail. But who?

The only person I was involved with physically was Nash. It could also be referring to my roommates, but what were the chances of that? I couldn't exactly stop seeing him because he held a secret that I didn't want to get out.

I could feel my stomach churning as I realized the reality of my situation. Going to the authorities wouldn't do shit because all I had was some letters that could be a sick prank that someone was playing and the game with Nash was he said, she said, at best. Since I didn't know who they were talking about, I decided to keep playing this game with Nash for the time being. Until I had more clarity, I had no other choice.

A FEW DAYS LATER, I stared at my open textbook, not absorbing any of the words on the pages I was supposed to be reading. I couldn't concentrate, no matter how much I tried. Not even my medication had helped today.

"What's going on?"

Izzy's words cut through the fog my brain was in and I turned to look at her. She, Lila, and I had decided to do our homework together in our living room. While they seemed to be getting a lot done, I, on the other hand, was mostly staring into space, lost in a daydream. Or was it a nightmare?

"It probably has something to do with a certain football player this town adores."

Lila's smirk deepened when my head turned toward her. "Looks like I was right," she said in a singsong voice.

"Where did you hear that from?" I didn't bother to confirm or deny her claim.

"People talk."

"I'm going to need you to give me more than that." I glanced at Izzy and found her staring at Lila. It seemed as if she was in the dark as much as I was.

"The Brentson Bears won a football game like a month ago. Usually when they win, there are a shit ton of parties around campus. Like seriously, it isn't hard to find a party and the football players visit quite a few of them to celebrate with everyone. Nash stopped by one party for a short period of time before announcing that he had other plans he had to attend to. That made people talk because he has never done that."

"What I'm not understanding is how I am in any way, shape, or form involved in this."

"You're the only girl he's been seen around recently. That is also something new as well."

"But I haven't been around him..." My voice trailed off as I tried to think. We'd been doing our best to keep whatever this was quiet. Meeting up in the evenings, checking to see if anyone else was around, etc. I tried to rack my brain about who might have seen us and when it hit me, it took everything within me to maintain a straight face. I thought back to the SUV that Nash said he'd found near my apartment. Had someone been spying on me, and then started a rumor about Nash and me? The thought seemed way too extreme, but I didn't know what else to think.

I watched as Izzy connected the dots, just like I had a few days ago when I first received the second letter. Discreetly, I tapped her under the table so she wouldn't say anything to Lila. I choose to focus back on the conversation at hand to try not to raise any suspicions.

The other part of Lila's statement that I found intriguing was people thinking I was with Nash again and his change in habits. I couldn't ask about the SUV or speak about what I was thinking because it seemed too farfetched to say out loud, so I went with the next best thing. "He had a revolving door of women coming in and out of his place?"

Lila nodded, and Izzy joined her. There was so much I didn't know about Nash in the years that we spent apart, and it was interesting learning more about it now. Part of me felt dejected by the confirmation of this suspicion, but I had no right to be. It didn't surprise me that he had done this.

Nash changing up his routine since I got here was more interesting. It also confirmed what I thought after showering at his place the night of the football game. He texted me after the game instead of hanging out with his teammates and not another woman. He still hated me or at least acted as if he did. Now I wondered if that was also a lie.

When my phone vibrated against the table, I knew who it was without looking. It was as if us talking about him had summoned him up from the depths of hell. I debated whether I wanted to look at the message. Apparently, I was a masochist because I snatched my phone off the table and read the text.

Nash: ***Come to my place in an hour.***

"DROP TO YOUR KNEES."

I folded my arms across my chest. "You could say please."

"There's no fun in that."

"Who said any of this was fun?"

"What did I tell you about lying?"

I bit the corner of my lip to keep from smiling, but I didn't move my body to abide by his order. "Say please."

His eyes grew dark, and I knew what that meant. I watched as his hand made its way from his side and to the back of my neck. He wrapped his hand around my ponytail and pulled back, tilting my head up and forcing me to look into his eyes.

"Drop. To. Your. Knees."

His tone this time was much different than before. This was all business, meant to show who was in control here. It sent a thrill through my body. He loosened his grip on my hair, and this time, I followed his directions and slowly kneeled on his carpeted floor.

What was I becoming? Who was this person?

We were getting further into the semester, and I couldn't count on both of my hands how many times we'd seen each other over the last few weeks. It felt as if I'd seen his bedroom about the same amount that I'd seen my own. The sex had been fantastic with no end in sight, which both excited and worried me.

Having great sex was no hardship on my part, even if it came from a guy who couldn't stand me. Maybe to the outside looking in, I should have higher standards, but I knew what this was and expected nothing else. What I didn't like was not having an expiration date, and I planned to ask him tonight... after this.

I leaned forward and lowered the gray sweats that I would have sworn on everything he'd worn for my benefit. His cock sprung forth and before either of us could make a sound, I took a hold of him in my hand.

Licking the head of his cock was my first move. I looked up and found Nash watching me with an intensity that both frightened me and made my pussy clench. I was so entranced by the reaction my body was having to playing with his dick that I stopped moving.

When his eyes opened, I saw something else in them, something outside of the hate I'd grown used to seeing. What was shining in them was pure ecstasy. The fact that I'd driven him there was... liberating.

But the look only lasted for a second. The hatred he felt for me filled his eyes, and then he said, "Did I tell you that you could stop?"

"No."

He raised one of his brows, daring me to continue. I grasped him again and took him in my mouth. My eyes met his again, but this time I didn't stop. Excitement pulsated through me as I watched his head fall back and his hand made its way into my hair, more than likely messing up my ponytail. Once I got used to taking his length, he tested his boundaries by pushing farther and farther into my mouth.

I gagged once as my reflex took over and he pulled back. To be honest, I was surprised he took that much care in making sure that he didn't go too far.

"Oh fuck, little bird."

This time, the nickname didn't sound like a death sentence. Hearing it fall from his lips while he is in this state served as nothing but encouragement. I enthusiastically sucked his cock until he took over and fucked my face. I grasped his thighs in order to keep steady because at the pace he was going, I would have fallen over.

His thrusts became haphazard instead of measured, telling me he was getting close. When he suddenly stopped moving, I braced for his release. I looked up at him just before he came and found him with his eyes closed, enjoying every last second of it.

Nash came with a loud groan and I couldn't help but wonder if it would turn into a roar.

I swallowed every drop and sat back on my heels as he took a step back. Based on what I observed, I had doubts about whether he could stand up straight after that. I shifted my body so I could stand up and walked over to grab a washcloth that Nash had placed on his bedside table when I walked into his bedroom. Once again, he was always prepared or thinking two steps ahead of everyone else.

I cleaned myself off as Nash pulled up his sweats. It was the first time he'd shown signs of being present since the blowjob.

I cleared my throat and asked, "When is this all going to end?"

He seemed taken aback by my question. "Huh?"

Maybe I shouldn't have asked him after I short-circuited his brain. "When is whatever this is going to end? I'm fulfilling my obligations just like we agreed."

"It ends when I say it does."

I jerked my head back in surprise. "That's not good enough for me."

"None of this is about you, Goodwin."

The harshness of his words hit me like a brick. It was obvious I hadn't done a good job of preparing myself for a negative response to my question when I should have known.

My feelings were written on my face. There was no way I was going to be able to mask any of my emotions from him, given the level of shock I was currently feeling.

It took a second for me to shake off the surprise before I said, "Look, Nash, this isn't—"

I knew when the idea appeared in his mind because his eyes lit up. "You're going to attend an event that is being held at my parents' house with me next week, and I'll have an end date for you by then."

I wrapped my arms around myself and turned to walk toward the window. This apartment wasn't placed in the center of New York City's skyline, but it still had a pretty view.

"Do I have a say in this?"

"No."

I didn't have much of a choice, but I wasn't going down without a fight. "Then no. I will not be going anywhere with you."

"Goodwin, this wasn't a question. You will be attending the party at my parents' house."

"No, I won't. It's not a good idea to be around your parents," I said.

"And why is that?"

"You know why and it doesn't bear repeating."

He clenched and unclenched his fist. The bliss he felt from the blow job seemed to be fading rapidly by the second, but that wasn't surprising, given the subject matter we were discussing.

"I think bringing you to my parents is the best idea I've had all day. I'll send you the location and other instructions soon."

His words made me flip around and stare at him with my mouth slightly agape. "Can you say that again?"

Nash looked at me strangely before he repeated what he said. His phrasing was a little strange to me and made me immediately think of the two hand-delivered letters I'd received.

Could he be the one sending me those notes? Had he forced me back to Brentson?

That realization hit me fast enough to make me swallow hard. Before my head could put together what was going on, I fled the room, hoping to put some distance between me and him. I ran into his bathroom and shut the door behind me, making sure to lock it to keep Nash out. Or at least trying to keep him out.

I turned on the faucet and sprayed my face with some water to cool down. As I dried my face off with a hand towel, there was a knock on the bathroom door.

I stared at the door, wondering if I didn't answer, would he snatch the door off its hinges. I jumped slightly when I heard him knock again. It sounded harder this time, vibrating the door. He was making sure I'd heard him this time or was losing patience with the current situation. Or both.

I glanced at the doorknob once more before I reached over and unlocked it. If he wanted to come in here, he could open the damn door himself. I wasn't surprised when he had no issue letting himself in.

"What happened?" It almost sounded like he gave a fuck.

I took a deep breath and said, "Nothing. I needed some time to myself."

I wanted to tell him that I panicked and was freaking out about his demand and that someone was forcing me to be at Brentson under the guise of telling me what happened to my mother.

When I tried to walk around Nash, he grabbed my arm, pulling me to within a breath of him. "You'll arrive at my apartment at the time I tell you to next weekend unless you want me to tell this whole fucking town what you did."

I snatched my arm out of his grip and glared at him. He was still the same asshole that he'd turned into after he graduated from high school. No matter how much I wished I was wrong, I knew I couldn't trust him.

21

NASH

"This is a bit much, isn't it?"

I looked up from my phone and found Raven walking out of the bathroom to stand in front of me. She was in the gown I selected for her to wear tonight.

I held back what I really wanted to say as I studied how the dress hugged her curves. Instead, I looked back down at my phone and said, "It's not. It's perfect for tonight's event."

"Mr. Henson?" I looked up again and turned to see who was holding some of the fabric behind Raven. "I'll have to make some minor adjustments, but I'll have it here an hour before you're planning on leaving."

I nodded and gave a small smile to the woman. Raven glared at me before turning around and walking back into the bathroom.

Asking Raven to attend a dinner at my parents' home hadn't been in the cards when I initially thought of my revenge plot against her, but here we were. They were throwing a party for some "close family and friends" as rumors spread that he was considering a run for governor. To be honest, I think it was just an excuse to throw a party, but I couldn't really blame them for that.

The seamstress left with the dress in hand, and Raven and I were soon alone again. She threw herself into a chair in the corner of the room and pulled out her phone. If she intended to ignore me for now, so be it, but she wouldn't be able to ignore me for long. I'd let her bide her time, but soon the only attention she would want, the only attention she would crave, would be from me.

My television played in the background, and neither of us said a word. I mindlessly watched the show that was playing and out of the corner of my eye, I saw her place her phone down and begin watching too. We'd watched about four shows when there was a knock on the door.

"Is that the dress? She finished making adjustments quickly."

I was surprised Raven said anything at all. Instead of answering her, I walked over to the door and opened it. In walked two women with huge smiles on their faces.

"Mr. Henson, we are here to do Raven's makeup and hair."

I don't think I've ever been called Mr. Henson this much in my entire life. I gave each woman a warm smile and said, "Come right this way."

When I turned around, I found Raven with her mouth hanging open. She recovered quickly and turned to me with a glare. It was a surprise to no one that she would still be irritated with me even when I've hired almost an army of people to make this happen tonight.

I walked over to her as the women who'd just arrived set up their equipment. "You can thank me later."

I didn't give her an opportunity to respond before I

walked out of the room. There was no way in hell I was going to tell her my plans before I did them. She would have argued with me, and while I did like sparring with her, now wasn't the time or place. I debated whether it was worth turning on the television in my bedroom or finding something else to do before I had to start getting ready when my phone rang.

With a sigh, I answered the phone because I knew if I didn't, he would keep calling.

"Yes, Dad?"

"Your mother said you're bringing a date to the party?"

That required a phone call? He'd see us in a couple of hours, which I couldn't wait for. The look on his face was going to be perfect, and I could hardly wait.

"I am."

"Excellent. We'll have to make sure to take photos. I want something that will end up getting statewide attention. It might end up making national news."

"There's always a chance of that, seeing as how so many things go viral nowadays." I said it as if I didn't have a care in the world, when in reality, my mind was racing about how tonight could go.

"Okay, I'll let you finish getting ready. See you soon."

"Later."

I hung up the phone with a new determination to set the scene for the fireworks that were sure to erupt tonight.

"You could have picked something that showed a little less cleavage."

Raven's voice carried as I walked into the living room

and saw her all dressed up for the first time. I couldn't help but stare. The last time I had seen her in something like this was at our prom. I then turned to look at her and focused most of my attention on her breasts before my eyes landed on her face. There was no doubt in my mind as she was the most beautiful person I'd ever laid my eyes on, even if there was no chance of me ever forgiving her. She wore a black gown that fit her like a glove with a slit up one leg. Her dark hair was in loose curls that rested just below her shoulders. The dress was sleeveless, so I bought her a black coat that she could wear over it because it was chilly outside.

The corner of my lips twitched. "Why? The designer literally made this gown for you."

I turned my attention away from her and reached over to grab my car keys that I'd haphazardly thrown on my kitchen counter. Since I didn't want to get stuck at my parents' house without an escape plan in case things went south, I decided that I was going to drive there tonight.

My comment took her by surprise based on the widening of her eyes and her mouth dropping open. Good. I liked to keep her on her toes.

"This is not a custom-made dress."

I shrugged and that's the only response she was going to get on the matter. It was made for her, and I'd only contacted the designer last week to make all of this happen.

I pulled a black velvety box out of my pocket and handed it to Raven. She raised an eyebrow at me before she opened it. When she saw what was inside, she snapped it back shut.

"Is this a game?"

"What's going on between us is *my* game." I gestured

between the two of us. "But what's in that box is not. I'll put it on you."

I took the box out of her hand and opened it again. Inside lay a bracelet full of diamonds and the chain was made of white gold. Raven hesitated before holding her wrist out. Her arm slightly shook as I put the bracelet on her. If she was nervous now, she definitely didn't want to know how much that bracelet cost me.

I stared at the bracelet for another second, admiring how it looked on her wrist. I shook my head as I helped her into her coat and then walked over to my front door. Once it was opened, I let her walk out first, with me following behind her. My eyes found their way to her ass, and I couldn't help but watch as her hips swayed even more than normal because of the heels she was wearing.

I led her down to my car, helped her inside, and then took off down the street toward my parents' home. The ride was mostly in silence, which I wouldn't lie and say I didn't appreciate.

Raven nervously fidgeted with her gown as I drove up to my parents' home on the outskirts of Brentson. Being this far out allowed them to have as much land as possible, ensuring that they wouldn't have to deal with nosy neighbors and other shenanigans as they referred to it. Thankfully, it wasn't too far out from the public or else mine and my sister's childhoods would have been quite lonely.

It did not surprise me to find that my parents had hired a valet service for the evening. As soon as I put my car in park, two men in suits opened the car doors for Raven and me. Several other people were helping other guests out of their cars and trying to make sure that the traffic kept flowing at a reasonable rate. This was one of the biggest parties that would be taking place in Brentson in recent memory, and everyone was abuzz with the rumors about my father's political future. It was also another way for my parents to boast about how much money they had without actually saying how much money they had.

I walked around my car and held out my arm for Raven to take before I led her up the stairs to the house. She was holding on to my arm for dear life and I slightly regretted putting her in this position. She hadn't asked for this, but I hadn't asked for her to do what she did to me either. Tonight would cause fireworks and I was going to have a front-row seat.

I'd intentionally made sure that I arrived late. It would be interesting to see how much of a reaction I would get given that there were so many people around.

I handed her coat to an attendant that my parents had hired for the night before putting my hand on the small of Raven's back and guided her into my childhood home.

"Not much has changed since I was last here," Raven said after she leaned toward me. The heels gave her an extra couple of inches, and I couldn't help but wonder how that would change the angle at which I fucked her.

Before I could answer, I saw my father's salt and pepper hair in the crowd. "We're going this way, Goodwin."

She squeezed my arm unnecessarily tight, letting me know just how much she didn't like me calling her by her last name.

I helped guide Raven through the crowd and saw my father standing next to my mother and sister, who'd been so kind as to grace us with her presence. I assumed they bribed her to be here with a smile on her face.

My mother spotted me first. She smiled at me, and then her gaze reached Raven. Her eyes widened to the point that I thought they might pop out of her head. That drew the attention of my father and sister, who had very different reactions to Raven's presence here.

Bianca, my sister, was more shocked than anything, but soon her lips broke out into a grin. As predicted, my father had the opposite reaction. His face was turning red in anger, and I loved every second. He was doing his best to maintain the calm politician exterior that he usually held together in public. We reached them before he had a chance to walk up to me.

"Nash, can I speak to you in private?"

It was getting harder to fight my smile. "No, because you wouldn't want to leave your guests now, would you?"

That left us in a stalemate, and I could feel Raven clinging to me even more. I could understand why she was nervous. Deep down, I knew bringing her here was a mistake, but I had to one-up him when I had the opportunity.

It was clear by the shiftiness in his eyes that he wanted to explode but couldn't, and I couldn't help but be ecstatic.

"How dare you bring her—"

"Watch how you refer to her..."

"Mayor Henson?"

All of us turned and found a staffer holding out a microphone to my father.

"It's time for you to make your speech."

Van Henson had never been in a situation where he couldn't charm the hell out of someone, but I wasn't sure if his charms would work over this crowd tonight if he couldn't get it together.

"We'll talk about *this* after."

I said nothing as he walked away with my mother trailing behind him. My sister gave me a thumbs up before she followed my mom, but I made sure that Raven and I stayed put.

Because we wouldn't be talking about this after. Hell, I wasn't even staying to hear his speech. As soon as he was almost to the area in our living room where I knew he loved to speak when he hosted people here, I pulled Raven by the hand and led her toward the stairs.

I hadn't been expecting for us to leave this soon, but it was for the better. And the best was only yet to come. As I led Raven down the hallway to my childhood bedroom, I couldn't help but think that if the fireworks I'd set off downstairs were anything, the ones that were about to occur up here would be a million times as powerful.

I felt my phone vibrate in my pocket. When I took it out, I was greeted by another text from an unknown number.

Unknown Number: ***Good job. Even I wouldn't have pulled off something this conniving.***

Who the fuck is this?

22

RAVEN

On our way to Nash's parents', I was nervous as fuck and kept adjusting the gown that he'd chosen for me to wear tonight. Between not being completely comfortable in such fancy clothes and later finding out that this gown was made for me, it was too much. I ran my hand over the black velvet again, relishing the feel of the fabric between my fingertips. It served the purpose of proving to me that all of this was real even though it felt as if I was veering between a dream and a nightmare.

I didn't know what Nash had planned before we got here and while today had been a wonderful experience in terms of getting pampered for the event, the drama he'd caused at his parents' had turned the entire night upside down. Not that I'd expected anything else from the Nash I knew now outside of longing for the relationship we shared when we were in high school.

He put his hand on my lower back just before he led me up the main stairs of his parents' home, I couldn't help but be taken down memory lane. I'd been to his home on numerous occasions while we'd been together. But this instance was completely different than any other time I'd been here.

"Where are we going?" I whispered as I looked behind us, wondering if someone was following me.

"Going to my bedroom."

I swallowed hard. "Why is that? Shouldn't we be leaving?"

"There's something I need to do."

Before I could ask any more questions, we reached his bedroom door. He hastily opened the door and when I hesitated for a second, he gently applied pressure to my lower back, forcing me to walk into the room before he locked the door behind us. Nash walked around me and walked over to a set of doors that led out to the balcony. He pulled the doors open with such force I thought he might snatch the door off its hinges.

"Go on, little bird. Step outside." He gestured to the doors. The look in his eyes told me exactly what he had in mind.

"Is something wrong with you? It's freezing out there!"

Nash chuckled, but it was anything but friendly. "I'm not here to play any games with you. Do it or I'll rip this dress off of you. Seam. To. Seam."

My legs followed his command before my brain could digest what he'd said. He smirked as I walked past him, but it quickly turned wicked. I ended up with both of my hands on the railing that protected anyone who stepped out here.

Nash followed me outside and crowded my body against the railing. "We're going to bring the house fucking down."

I didn't doubt him for a moment, but there was no way I was getting naked right here. Anyone could see, especially if they had a camera or heard us.

"Lift up the back of your dress."

I shivered and I wasn't sure if it was due to the temperature outside or his words. I grasped the fabric of the dress in my hand and pulled it up, exposing my ass to him.

"Red this time... my favorite color. Spread your legs."

It seemed as if at least one thing hadn't changed since I'd left Brentson. And I'd used that knowledge to my advantage when choosing what I wanted to wear under this gown tonight.

I moved my legs as I heard what sounded like him unzipping his pants. He used his hand to force me to lean forward and I felt his finger run up and down my pussy. I didn't want to lean into his finger, but my body wouldn't be denied.

"You're soaked and I haven't done anything yet. Fuck..." His voice trailed off as if entranced by my arousal. "The idea of being caught turns you on, doesn't it?"

I nodded my head, not even bothering to deny his claim. I groaned as his finger continued to play with me and I let my dress fall where it may.

"Tell me what you want."

I didn't trust my voice to properly relay my opinion. I was too far into the sensations he was inflicting on my body.

"Little bird, I'm going to stop what I'm doing if you don't tell me what you want."

I knew he had no problem denying me what I desperately needed, so I wasted no more time. "I want you to fuck me."

"There are many ways I could fuck you. I'm going to need for you to be more specific."

"I want you to... fuck me with your fingers, and then your cock." I hated how I sounded, but I was frantic for his touch.

"You're so fucking greedy."

For any part of him I was, apparently.

I should have been embarrassed to have my ass exposed like this, but if it made it easier for Nash to fuck me, I couldn't care less. I could feel him pull my thong to the side, and then he finally gave me what I wanted and pushed his finger into my pussy. My eyelids shut, heightening the rest of my senses as he drummed up my arousal.

This angle was different from anything I'd ever experienced and soon thoughts of whether or not I would fall over this railing or if anyone could see or hear what we were doing fell away. All that mattered was that I had this man, right here, right now, prepared to fuck me into the next universe.

My eyes opened as I grounded against his hand as I tried to get even closer to him when we were only a breath apart.

"You love how I treat your sweet cunt, don't you?"

I nodded my head like a bobble head doll, hoping that this would encourage him to keep the pace he was going.

"Use your words, Goodwin."

His shift from the nickname he gave me when we were kids and the bite that surrounded every syllable of my last name was like whiplash.

"I love how you..." I failed to complete my sentence.

"What was that?"

"I-I love how you treat my sweet cunt."

"And when you're old and gray, you're still going to be thinking about how I fucked you so hard in plain damn sight."

His words were a damper on my mood, but I didn't have time to dissect my feelings. Nash snatched his finger out of my pussy, and, in a blink, I heard a condom wrapper rip. His dick took the place of his finger before he impaled me on his cock. I cried out, not caring if anyone who might have stepped outside for a quick break might have heard me.

He reached from behind me and grabbed my neck, anchoring me in place. The pressure he was placing on my neck wasn't enough to make me suffocate but having his hand around my throat while he pounded into me made me even wetter.

I groaned as he continued and reached behind me to place my hand on his leg, encouraging him to slam into me harder. I froze in place when I heard something below us. My entire body clenched, and Nash moaned, his cock still inside of me. It was then I heard the soft voices of two women below us. I couldn't make out what they were saying, but it was obvious that we weren't alone.

"Do you hear those people down there?" Nash asked, having slowed his movements.

I dreaded saying the words and I couldn't control how quickly they fled my mouth. "I do. We need to stop before they—"

He pounded into me, effectively shutting me up. My hands muffled the squeal that almost came out as he charged into me once more.

And he didn't stop.

My hand covered my mouth while trying to avoid Nash's hold on my neck. I silently prayed that they wouldn't look up and see what was going on, but that was with no help from Nash. He was determined to make sure that everyone in Brentson heard him driving me to the brink of my sanity.

There was no way the people below us didn't hear what was occurring just above their heads. Between the sounds as our bodies came together, my struggle to maintain my moans, and Nash's grunts, there's no way they couldn't hear what was going on.

They took their time getting some fresh air as Nash continued to fuck me from behind. My mind drifted from the people who'd stepped outside back to the ecstasy Nash was forcing through my body. Another moan left my lips and this time, my hand didn't do a good job of protecting it.

"That's it. You can't hold back how fucking fantastic this feels. Your pussy has a chokehold on my cock." He punctuated his statement by ramming into me again.

My breath caught in my throat, and I prayed that the people below us would leave. There was no way I was going to be able to last much longer if he kept up with this pace.

As if they heard my pleas, I heard their voices fade and when I couldn't hear their voices anymore, I screamed out, not caring who heard me. I expected him to say something slick, but he didn't. I heard him mumble a cuss word as he grew closer to coming undone.

Hearing his desperation for his release was what sent me over the edge and sent me careening out of control like a runaway car. There was no controlling my body as my climax slid through me. Thankfully, I was sandwiched between Nash and the balcony's railing, or I was sure my body would have ended up falling to the ground.

My orgasm did nothing to slow Nash down. In fact, it fed into his desperateness to reach his own climax. His thrusts became reckless, like he couldn't get enough of me or the connection we shared. I didn't blame him because the sex between us was addicting as fuck.

When he pulled away, I did my best to fix my clothes while I heard some rustling behind me. I didn't turn around because I was too embarrassed by what we'd done out here. And by how much I enjoyed it.

I heard Nash approach me again and I shivered. He walked up to me and put his hands on my shoulders.

"Not once did you mention the chill in the air," he whispered in my ear as he fixed the back of my gown.

I hadn't, because my body felt as if it were on fire from what he'd done to me. It was almost like I was in a haze and my body was still having an issue catching up to the events that had just occurred.

Nash spoke again and I fought hard to concentrate on his words. "By the way, I never would have let anyone see what was mine."

I thought back to when he said he would have ripped my dress if I hadn't complied with his demand and now I knew that was a lie.

Together we walked back downstairs and toward the front door to grab my coat. Once it was retrieved, he placed my hand in his and we went outside where he handed the valet his ticket. While we waited for his car to be driven around, I couldn't help but feel I'd finally found my footing in this fucked-up situation.

23

RAVEN

I tapped my foot as I waited for the clock to reach seven. I fought my yawn again, unable to fight the tiredness that was making its presence known. Why did this evening seminar have to be a thing?

Thankfully, this wasn't a common occurrence because there was no way I'd be able to do this weekly. I'd also made sure to take my medication to ensure I would be able to focus and take notes.

I checked my phone as if that would make the time move faster. At least there were only five minutes to go. I tried my best to pay attention for the last few minutes, but I was the first one up as soon as my professor dismissed us. There had been some hair pulling by me during the talk, but I'd survived.

It didn't take me long to pack my backpack and when I stood up, I looked toward the top of the lecture hall and found Landon looking at me. Before I could react, he turned on his heel and rushed out of the room. *What the hell was that all about?*

There were too many people standing around for me to run after him and when I finally made it to the exit, he was nowhere to be found. I jogged out of the building and couldn't find him but instead of wandering around, I dashed to my car. The ride back home was effortless and as soon as I opened my front door, I let out the loudest sigh ever. My mind was still on seeing Landon staring back at me and the whole thing didn't sit well with me.

"That bad, eh?"

I found Lila and Erika sitting on the couch, watching a movie and snacking on the popcorn between them.

"Yeah, I just found out evening classes aren't for me."

"Did you take any before you transferred back here?" Erika's question was a valid one.

"I took courses online. If we had any live sessions, they were during the day and I'm used to doing homework in the evenings, but attending a class at night? That takes way more brain power than I have, I think. I turn into a pumpkin by five p.m."

That caused both girls to chuckle.

Lila looked over at me before looking back at the television screen. "Do you want to watch this movie with us? We only started it twenty minutes ago."

"No, thanks. I think I'm just going to get in the shower, and then go to bed. I'll see you both later."

I left Lila and Erika in the living room and went into my bedroom. It took less than two minutes to hop into the shower. There was nothing like washing a long day away.

I didn't know how much time had passed before I'd stepped out of the shower and tightened my towel around my body. All I wanted to do now was to crawl into bed.

My phone's screen lit up, and I rushed over to it. I rolled my eyes when I saw it was a text from Izzy.

Izzy: ***Did our landlord come by to check out the leak from the bathroom sink?***

Me: ***Yes. He came by when I had a break between classes and he was in and out within ten minutes.***

Izzy: ***Thank you!***

I didn't roll my eyes because Izzy was texting me to check in on something that our landlord was supposed to help us with. I rolled my eyes at myself because I was hoping it was Nash that was sending me a message.

I hadn't heard from Nash since he'd dropped me off at home directly after the event at his parents' house. The scene there was enough to make anyone want to go bury themselves in a hole. However, Mayor Henson still hadn't announced his intentions and none of that explained why Nash hadn't contacted me about this "game." Every time I got a text message, I suspected it was from him and when I realized it wasn't, tension fled my body. Then I was back to being on edge as I found myself waiting for his next move.

I slowly got dressed in my pajamas, and after some difficulty, put the bracelet Nash gave me back on my wrist. It wasn't something I would have picked out for myself, but it was a lovely piece of jewelry that reminded me of Nash.

While this whole arrangement wasn't normal, his behavior now was even stranger, and I was left wondering what the hell was going on. Calling him would be odd and would make it seem like I wanted him.

But you fucking do, Raven.

I didn't like the way he treated me, but there were these moments that made me think differently. Sure, we weren't out in the open like we were in high school, but his caring nature was breaking through and reminded me of the boy that I used to know. The one who loved the sight of me, the one who would make sure I had everything I needed.

Just as I finished tossing my hair into a ponytail, my text message alert played loudly. When had I turned it on? I must have hit a button when I was texting Izzy. I turned my phone back to vibrate and my heart jumped when I saw it was from Nash. It was as if he'd known I was thinking about him. Then again, when wasn't I thinking about him these days?

I sat down on the edge of my bed and read the message.

Nash: ***Meet me at my place tonight at 9 p.m. Alone.***

I couldn't stop myself from typing my reply.

Me: ***Alone? Isn't that the only way I go to your apartment?***

I waited a beat and when I didn't get a response, I typed a follow-up message.

Me: ***Nash, what the hell is going on?***

When he didn't respond to that, I threw my hands in the air and rolled my eyes. I couldn't help but be curious about why he mentioned me being alone.

This was a feeling I couldn't shake. I stared at his message for a second too long before I tried calling his number. It immediately went to voice mail.

Nash: ***Can't talk right now. See you tonight.***

His text back settled some of the tension I felt, but it drew up another feeling in my mind.

Even with the shitty way he'd treated me since our reunion, deep down, I wanted him. I craved the way we were when we were kids and the way he would treat me when his mask would temporarily slip. If he needed to tell the secret that he'd been holding over me for the last few weeks, then so be it. If this didn't go anywhere after we talked, then so be it. But I couldn't keep this charade up.

He'd only given me a small part of him this time around, and I knew this. What was fucked up about it was that I wanted whatever he would give. This sounded toxic as hell, yet I couldn't break the hold he had on me. That was even with the warning that he would end this at any time and any place of his choosing.

I could sit here and not go, but I wanted to find out what happened after I'd left him last. I shoved aside my pride and walked over to my closet to find something to wear tonight.

24

NASH

"One more time!"

I wanted to tackle Easton, but that would risk injuring one of us and Coach would have no problem murdering me.

I ran through the drill again before I waved Easton off. I wasn't exhausted physically, but I didn't want to do this drill again.

"Done?" Easton asked as he walked over to me.

"Yeah, man. I'm done." I nodded, and he tossed me the football.

"Did that help you get out the stick you've had up your ass for the last week?"

I shoved Easton hard and all he did was chuckle. "I feel better."

"Better enough to text Raven? Maybe she can pull the stick out."

"You don't ever shut up, do you?"

Easton shrugged. "You should know that I don't by now."

I shook my head and went over to my gym locker. I grabbed the things I needed before heading home. The last thing I wanted to be thinking about was Raven, but thanks to Easton, now I was.

That was a lie. I'd been thinking about her since the moment I saw that she was back in Brentson.

I thought about her my entire drive home. When I walked into my apartment, I dropped my gym bag at the door and pulled out my cell phone. I hadn't texted her over the last week because I didn't want to be bothered. There was enough to deal with right now between avoiding my father, football, and the Chevaliers' shit.

But not having her around was affecting my mood. The "game" we were playing was an outlet for me. A way to exact revenge and a way to fuck her into submission.

Maybe it was time to send her a text.

I pulled out my phone to send the text when someone knocked on my front door. I stood still and wondered if the person would leave if they thought no one was home. Then there was another knock.

"Nash! I know you're in there!" My father's voice reverberated through the closed door.

Just because he knew I was in here didn't mean I had to answer the door. Sure, he'd also cosigned on this apartment, but I couldn't care less.

Then again, not handling this head-on would seem cowardice on my part. I'd been dodging his calls for days and maybe it was time for the finale of this showdown.

I tossed my phone to the side and walked over to my front door. When I opened it, a shocked expression flashed on my father's face for a second before anger returned. It looked as if he was surprised I opened the door at all.

"What do you want?" That was the only greeting he was going to get. Instead of replying, he shoved past me. I shrugged and closed the door behind me.

Once we heard the door click shut, my father spun around and said, "How dare you bring that... girl to my party!"

"I didn't find anything wrong with it. You said if I wanted to bring a date, I could. So, I did."

"You knew better than to bring her!"

"I wasn't given any qualifications that my date needed to have, so I brought who I wanted."

I smiled to myself because I could see how agitated he was becoming. I was stoking his anger, and nothing right now could give me more joy. It served him right.

"Cut the bullshit, Nash."

I'd had enough of this, and his time here was rapidly coming to a close. "No, you cut the bullshit. The fact that you are still pissed about this days later literally makes no sense. I showed up for your stupid party and that was all you asked me to do. It was successful. You got your photos, and you are still dragging people along even though everyone knows you're running for governor."

"You brought her there on purpose to cause trouble and you know it."

"The reason she was there was to be my date. Any other ideas you had about her presence there is not my concern. Now if you'll excuse me, I have things to do for the Chevaliers."

I didn't have anything to do for them right now, but I knew that by saying it, he'd leave. He wanted me to succeed where he failed in his quest to become one of the leaders of this chapter, so I knew it was a button that could be pressed to get him to back off.

I watched as the tension released from his body. It was so easy to shift his mind to other matters, especially when any sort of reference to more power was involved.

"Early morning tomorrow?"

"Yes, so I'll see you later?"

"Fine. I assume you'll be coming home at some point to see your mother and Bianca."

"I will."

"And we will talk about this, but I don't want to distract you from..." His voice trailed off, and I knew he was referring to the trials.

I walked him to the front door and once he left, I shut it behind him.

Talking to him made my mind up. I was going to hop in the shower, and then drive over to Raven's house. What I needed to work out of my system now was something only she could fix.

About an hour later, I drove to Raven's house, and to my surprise, there was a black SUV parked in front of her driveway, blocking her car in. I parked across the street and checked the time: 8:34 p.m.

I took my seat belt off and before I could make a move to

step out of the car, I watched as Raven's house door opened. When I saw it was her, I got out of the car and that was when everything went to hell. The driver's side door of the SUV opened, and I saw him jump out of the vehicle. I reacted without another thought.

Raven screamed as he grabbed her, but all of that stopped when I tackled him to the ground. Once I got a handle on him, I yelled at Raven, "Grab my car keys and open the trunk!"

I suspected she was in too much shock to do anything else but follow my directions. I grabbed the asshole and when he looked as if he was going to say something, I punched him, distracting him enough that he wouldn't start yelling and draw even more attention to us.

"Raven, I have zip-ties in my glove compartment. Grab them."

When she looked as if she might argue with me, I glared at her, shutting her up as well. She did as I asked, then I zip tied the would-be kidnapper and threw him into my trunk.

I slammed the door down and said, "Get into the car now!"

Raven ran toward the passenger door and before she could snap her seat belt into place, I took off down the street.

Things only grew more tense when the fucker in my trunk started making noise and tried to yell.

"Shut the fuck up!" I yelled and pressed my foot down on the gas pedal.

Raven screamed next to me and grasped her seat belt. "You kidnapped someone!"

"Who was about to kidnap you, so it cancels out."

"What the hell is wrong with you?"

Instead of giving her a verbal answer, I turned to glance at her. My grin took over my face. She didn't know the half of it.

There was no way I could take him back to my house, but I knew exactly where we could go.

25

RAVEN

If I thought I didn't recognize Nash when I came back to Brentson, I definitely didn't know who the man sitting next to me now was.

I couldn't put into words what was happening. Nash had kidnapped a man and now I was an accessory to the crime because I got into the car with him. He hadn't held me at gunpoint. I'd willingly gotten into the car with him. And now we were driving to who knows where, with someone who'd attacked me.

Nash pressed a button and called someone using his Bluetooth that was connected to the car. It rang until the person on the other end picked up.

"Yo," the person said.

"Meet me at the side door. I have a package."

He hung up before anything else was said and it left me looking at him like he'd absolutely lost his mind. Why would you refer to someone, a human being, as a package?

My heart was racing, and I couldn't think straight. Every

thought circled around to us being thrown in jail for what we were doing. "Nash, you need to stop this."

"I will."

But he made no motion to pull the car over or anything.

"This isn't stopping what's going on right now. We should go to the police." I felt around for my phone. *Shit. The guy in the trunk snatched it from me before he grabbed me.*

"Some things are better handled a different way," he said. The eeriness in his voice was downright frightening and I worried about my safety.

I tried to swallow my fears and talk to him calmly because I wasn't sure what he was capable of.

Stay calm, Raven. Stay calm.

I needed to keep a clear head, even though my thoughts were all over the place.

When he made a right turn, we ended up on a road that led to a long driveway. The driveway was connected to a large, older-looking building. It looked as if it might have been built around the time Brentson University was founded, but it looked well maintained from what I could see at night. It was a little creepy but nothing too surprising if it had been built when I thought it had been.

"Where are we?" My words left my mouth slowly because I didn't trust myself to be able to speak coherently.

"The Chevaliers' Manor."

My mouth dropped open as I thought about what Izzy said about the secret society that hardly anyone knew about. I thought about the freshman who was killed and his connection to this organization. Panic surged through me as I thought of all the things that could happen to me.

I needed to get out of here.

Nash parked his car near the side of the building, and two guys walked out. There was no way I was going to escape right now when I was outnumbered.

Nash popped the trunk, and then turned to me. "I'm going to take you to a room where you're to stay until I get you. Do you understand me?"

I nodded because I had no other choice. The two guys went to the trunk as Nash left the car and came around the front. His eyes never strayed from mine, as if daring me to pull some sort of stunt. He opened my car door and helped me out of the vehicle. It was nice to see he still maintained his manners even after kidnapping someone.

He led me to the house with his hand on my lower back, much like he had the evening he'd taken me to his parents' party. The home maintained the same atmosphere I'd noticed when we were outside. It was dimly lit, making it hard to make out everything, but I could see that it looked well-kept and clean. There were some portraits on the wall, but no one I could see clearly enough to identify. I assumed I wouldn't recognize them anyway if the historical feel this place was going for was true. We continued down the hall and I heard what I assumed was the guy who had been in the trunk of Nash's car started yelling.

"He can yell all he wants, but help isn't coming to save him."

"Why are you doing this?"

"Because he shouldn't have been stalking you."

I almost tripped over my two feet. "You think that was the guy you saw the other night on my block? Who drove in reverse down the street?"

"Yes, and I assume he's been stalking you for some time.

Maybe he felt more comfortable being more open about it once you were in the house. Or maybe this was the only location he was watching you at. Regardless, I think it was him and he was going to kidnap you tonight."

I gasped even though Nash's assumption was a complete surprise. I mumbled under my breath as Nash led me into a room and shut the door behind us. He turned on the light and that was the first time since we'd gotten here that I could see clearly where I was.

It looked to be a spare bedroom that contained a bed, a dresser, and a desk, much like you would see in your standard dorm room. The thought of taking a nap here made my skin crawl.

"Repeat that, Goodwin."

I rolled my eyes because it had become a habit with his constant need to refer to me by my last name. "The only reason I was outside was because I got a text from you saying you wanted to meet at your house at nine tonight. I was headed to my car when you ran up and... you know."

"Huh. I didn't text you. The only reason I was outside of your house and saw what was about to happen was because I was trying to surprise you."

As the pieces clicked together, I just stared at him. This couldn't be true, but everything that I knew about what was going on led up to this. "It was a setup."

"He must have spoofed my number in order to get you to think that it was me texting you. Good to know."

Nash walked over to me and before I could register what he was doing, he lifted my head so that he could kiss me. The kiss felt powerful and all-consuming and scrambled my brain even further about what was happening right now. Then he stepped away.

"I need to go but remember what I said: stay in this room until I come back for you."

I nodded. "I will."

He gave me another quick peck on the lips before he left me alone.

That was another promise that I had no intention of keeping.

26

NASH

Leaving Raven behind in the spare bedroom was something I wasn't fully comfortable with, but it needed to be done. I didn't want her witnessing what was about to happen. I made a mental note to myself to send one of the guys to make sure she didn't leave the room.

I raced through the house and found the stairs that would take me to the main floor because I knew where they had taken him. This wasn't the first time we'd taken someone to this special room, and it wouldn't be the last. Things were strangely quiet for this time of year, but it was perfect because that meant fewer people I had to tell what was going on.

The portraits of Chevaliers from years past guided me, fueling my rage to correct this situation. This fucker had touched what was mine and now he was going to pay for it.

I walked into one of the special rooms in Chevalier Manor. In this room, some people were allowed to experiment with different tools to get the answers that we wanted. Our lovely everyday stalker was tied to a chair.

"What's your name?"

"Paul."

"Okay, Paul. Who sent you to spy on Raven?"

"Who?"

"Don't even try this. The woman you were attempting to kidnap."

A sick smile appeared on his lips before he said, "Your mama."

"Oh, now we're doing your mama jokes. How clever."

"I thought so too."

I walked over to a cabinet and opened both doors. Inside of it were all types of guns, knives, and other types of weapons that we had at our disposal. I chose a machete and turned back around to find Raven's stalker staring at me, he was wide-eyed with fear. *Good.*

"Now, once again, who sent you to stalk Raven?"

He looked me in the eye and said, "I'm not saying anything."

"Why? Don't you value your life?"

He didn't speak a word.

I grabbed Paul by his collar and said, "Tell me who. Sent. You."

When he didn't respond again, I punched him. I was impressed by the amount of force that was behind my fist because I was still holding the machete.

"You can hit me as much as you want, but I'm not telling you who hired me."

I nodded slowly. "That makes a lot of sense, actually. One of you, hold his head and turn it to face the cabinet."

Once his head was held in place, I took the machete and pierced his skin from his hairline down to his neck.

His screams were like medicine for my soul.

"Who was it?"

"What part of *I'm not telling you* don't you understand, asshole! No matter what you do with me, I'm as good as dead anyway."

This man had nothing to lose. I was wasting my breath trying to get him to talk, but at least I was having fun.

I ran the machete down the back of his hand and although he tried to hold it together, he cried out.

"Tell me who sent you."

"No!"

"Fine." I gestured to the other Chevaliers in the room. "Strap his arms down too."

Paul fought against their hold but was soon restrained further. I wasted no more time. I ran the machete down the side of his head and enjoyed the blood that followed in its wake.

"Fuck you! Why are you doing this?"

I shrugged as I examined my handiwork. "Because you touched her."

He screamed again before he said, "Fucking idiot. You think you've won."

A small smile appeared on my face. "I don't *think* I've won. I know I have."

"That's where you are wrong. I'm just the beginning. And tell Raven Goodwin that she was warned."

"Warned by who?"

He refused to respond again, and I assumed it was due to his agony. At this point, he was boring me, and I'd had enough.

I pulled his head back and said, "I hope this hurts like

hell." Without another thought, I slit his throat and let his head flop lifelessly.

Someone quickly handed me a towel to wipe any blood off of me. It was then that I realized I was shaking, and I couldn't stop it.

It was without a doubt because of the adrenaline coursing through my body. I couldn't help but smile because I felt fantastic. I'd never thought I would get a thrill from murdering someone, yet here I was grinning after taking someone's life. Being in control about whether someone lived or died had a way of making you feel gleeful.

When I heard clapping coming from the other side of the room, I swung around and found Tomas standing there.

"Henson, you know you're supposed to seek approval before coming down here."

That was true. It was usually up to the chairman to decide if we were allowed to torture someone in the manor. "You knew I was down here, so if you wanted to stop me, you could have."

"True."

"He needed to be dealt with quickly. My motto is that it's better to ask for forgiveness than permission."

That caused Tomas to chuckle, which was rare. "Good job."

"You don't even know who he was or why I killed him."

"I have an idea. He messed with what's yours and that was his consequence. You chose courage and loyalty when you had plenty of other choices on the table and that was why you were always best suited to become an Eagle. This first part of the trial was never going to be a problem for you... but the rest... well, we'll see."

Tomas was right and that was what had driven my innate desire to make sure he didn't walk out of here alive. My killing of Paul showed my loyalty to Raven and displayed the qualities that they were looking for with someone who would be the future chairman.

The kicker was that I hadn't even done this with the Chevaliers in mind. The only thing on my mind had been Raven.

"This might have been the greatest thing you'll ever do."

I took his praise and smirked. "One of the greatest things I'll ever do is take your position when you graduate."

"Let's not get too far ahead of ourselves here," Tomas replied. "But this was an excellent step in that direction. Good work. Especially on keeping the mess to a minimum."

He reached out to shake my now somewhat clean hand. And when he walked away, my mind drifted to the person who occupied my thoughts constantly. I grabbed her phone that had been placed on a table near the entrance before I paused.

It was then that I realized I never sent someone back to the room that I told Raven to stay in.

27

RAVEN

My eyes widened as my hands flew to my mouth in an attempt to block any sounds. Nash and the other men in the room couldn't know that I was here or I might end up like the guy strapped to that chair, currently bleeding out. Apparently, that didn't matter.

Because when I saw Nash look in my general direction, I knew I was fucked unless there was a way that I could avoid being found.

I walked alongside the wall, hoping there wasn't anything that could trip me up and give away my location. My eyes were still trained on Nash, praying that he couldn't see me.

When he made no move my way, I risked taking my eyes off of him and found what could be a doorway, but I wasn't completely sure. The only choice I had was to find out because being found by Nash or any of the people that might be in this building wasn't an option I was willing to take. It was only a matter of time before he realized I'd escaped, and I didn't want to know what the repercussions of that would be.

I slowly made my way toward what I hoped was a doorway that would, at best, get me to the outside. At worst, it would lead me to more of the Chevaliers, who would have no problem delivering me back to Nash.

It took some maneuvering, but I made my way to what I confirmed was a doorway and dashed to the door. Although every inch of me wanted to yank the door open, I knew that the best approach was to not act too hastily. If this door was unlocked, I didn't know how noisy it would be or if it would alert anyone. I felt around and found the doorknob.

Without giving it a second thought, I pulled on it and when the door gave way, I could breathe again.

I was going to get out of here once I found the right door. That relief was short-lived because once I opened it, I realized the doorway didn't lead outside. It just led to a hallway full of doors.

Fuck.

The thought that I might die in here flashed before me as I tried another door. But this one didn't budge either. With every door that didn't open, my hopes were fleeing. I was running out of options.

I ran to another door and tried to open it. It didn't budge. I slammed my fist into the door in frustration and anger because I had been denied once again. It took everything in me to bite back the cussword that threatened to fall from my lips. I'd probably alerted whoever was in this fucked-up place to where I was, but I didn't have time to worry about that.

The next three doors I tried all had the same result. With each doorknob I turned that didn't budge, I saw my chances of getting out of here alive dwindling.

I pivoted before rushing to the last door, praying that this would be it. I used all my weight to push on the door in the never-ending hallway. If this didn't lead me to the outside world, any hope of making it out of here alive was dashed. When it opened under the weight of my hands, I almost screamed with glee into the crisp night air.

But I couldn't. Because then he would find me.

I took off, pumping my arms as fast as I could, hoping that they, along with my legs, would propel me forward. I glanced behind me once to see if I was being followed, but I couldn't tell. All that I knew was that I needed to keep running—even if my destination was unknown. Praying that the woods I ran through would provide enough coverage that I wouldn't be easy to find.

All I could do was focus on getting away from there. Getting away from that. Staying and hiding was an option, but it was far too risky. If they caught me, I knew they would kill me. Hell, if he caught me, I knew I would have the same fate.

My shoe caught on a branch and I tripped. It threw me off my stride and shook me to my core. I bit back a scream as I tried to catch myself. Thoughts rushed through my mind as I mentally took a beating before I recovered. I was afraid that the slight pause would end up costing me my life.

I raced ahead, ignoring the pain burning in my chest that came from how fast I was running. The remnants of snow on the ground didn't make this trek any easier. Would my limbs or lungs give out before I reached the road? Would I trip again? Why had I decided to come back to Brentson at all?

I mentally berated myself for coming to this school and back to this town. I left for a good reason, and I should have stayed gone.

Everything I knew was a lie. I was an idiot for falling for it because, once again, the only thing I could count on was myself.

I gasped when I saw a light up ahead. It gave me hope that I was getting closer and closer to civilization. Once I reached a road, I knew I could find out where I was. After all, I was born and raised in Brentson, New York. Returning to my hometown had unlocked wounds that I'd hoped were dead and buried.

Hometown? I'd left this place on a whim two years ago and only returned when I was summoned. I was promised that I would find out what happened to my mother. That, and a dark secret I wished to keep hidden were what kept me away, but my quest for closure had brought me back.

And now I was involved in this bullshit. Heavily involved. I was an eyewitness to a murder, and now I was worried that the murderer had turned his attention to me.

The light grew closer, and tears grew in my eyes, but I wasn't sad. I was so close to getting away. If I could just make it to what should be a road up ahead.

The chance at being free guided me, pushing me to keep my body propelling forward. I charged toward the streetlight that became closer and closer as my stride ate up the distance between me and it.

What would I do when I reached the clearing? Part of the battle was knowing where I was, the other was finding some form of help. But I would deal with that when I came to it. My phone would have been helpful right now, but I was sure that it was still on my kidnapper who snatched it when he was attempting to abduct me.

Knowing what I knew about Brentson and the

surrounding area, I could be anywhere. The only thing I knew was that I was near the Chevalier Manor, but where that was in relation to campus, I had no idea. I assumed that I might be still somewhat close to campus, further increasing the likelihood that I would find someone to help me.

But could anyone help me? After all, I couldn't tell anyone what had just occurred... or what all had happened since I stepped foot back into Brentson.

Brentson.

I was called back for a reason. That reason, I still didn't know, but they used my mother's death to lure me back here. I regretted opening the letter I received that started it all. The letter that brought me back here and had indirectly thrown me into all of this.

I was so close to the streetlight that it almost felt as if it were calling to me. Asking me to shed light on the darkness I had seen. Had experienced. That I continued to live in.

Yet, I couldn't. At least not yet.

My downfall was seeing Nash Henson again. The boy I'd fallen in love with had become a man hell-bent on revenge. He had every right to see it through.

Thoughts of him flew out of my brain when I reached the light I'd seen in the distance. Another tear fell down my cheek. I had found a street. I looked back to see if anyone had followed me, but all I could hear was the light whipping of the breeze as I leaned against the lamppost, I took in big gulps of air, hoping to catch my breath and calm my racing heart. Instead, all I could see was that I wasn't safe. Not by a long shot.

When I slowed my breathing down, I looked forward and behind me before I recognized the road I was on: State Street.

It seemed deserted, but that was to be expected at this time of night.

I shivered, but I wasn't sure if it was the cold air or the shock.

If I walked along the road, I would end up back on campus eventually, but I knew I had to worry about whoever the hell was still in the building I'd run from and anyone else who might want to capture me.

As I pushed off the light-post and rubbed my hands on the sweatshirt that did a decent job of protecting me from the elements, a car's headlights came toward me. My first instinct was to wave them down to see if they could help, but I noticed how slowly the car was driving. Almost as if its occupants were searching for something.

Me.

I ran back into the woods, hoping to conceal myself, but I didn't want to go too far from State Street. I found a tree that I thought was big enough to cover me completely and I stood still as I patiently watched the car drive past. Once I saw the red of the car's brake lights disappear, I breathed a sigh of relief. I didn't recognize the car. Maybe it was someone driving through town and trying to find their way in an unfamiliar place.

I waited a few beats to make sure that the car wasn't circling back around, and then I took off again, running in the direction of Brentson University. I didn't know what would greet me when I arrived back on campus, but I knew it had to be better than anything I'd just witnessed.

Or so I thought.

I'd been so focused on running toward campus, that I hadn't noticed the headlights until it was too late. To make matters worse, the headlights shone on the road just to the right of me. The car was driving on the wrong side of the road.

It would be a worthwhile bet for me to guess that the car I'd just seen moments ago had swung around and was patrolling my location once again.

The driver had seen me.

After a deep breath, I kept running, willing my body to not break down during this chase. But it was of no use. I was still exhausted from the run through the woods earlier and my hopes were dashed before my eyes. I paused as I tried to recover and figure out what the driver's next move was going to be. If this person was trying to catch me, they were well on their way to succeeding. But I wasn't out of options yet. I debated running deeper into the woods, but there was a chance I'd never get out alive. I glanced back at the car and kept walking, knowing deep down I was just prolonging the inevitable.

The car pulled to a stop several feet away from me, and I made another mental calculation—wondering again if it was worth attempting to run. As I was about to take off again, the driver spoke.

"Goodwin."

I stopped. My last name falling from his lips was enough to halt my tracks. I turned around and faced the man who would soon become my captor.

"Are you going to get in, or am I going to have to toss you into the trunk?"

Nash, the person who I once thought would be my savior from everything evil. Instead, he'd become Satan himself.

The urge to run again was still there, but I knew that as of now, the likelihood of me getting away was slim. I walked around the front of the car and slid into the passenger seat wearily. I made sure to sit as far away from Nash as I could as he pulled away from where he'd parked and continued down the dark road.

If I wasn't in a situation where I feared for my life or witnessed a murder, I could have laughed out loud at the events that had occurred tonight.

The thought that I was going to get away without issue was comical at this point. The events of the last couple of hours played on repeat in my mind while Nash drove us to who knows where. It had been foolish of me to think that getting out of Chevalier Manor would be that easy, but I would make the same decision that I made over and over again, even if it guaranteed the same result. I refused to just give in to the hand I'd been dealt, and this was no exception.

I would laugh at how quickly my fortune had turned, but all it would do was bring more attention from Nash. Maybe then he would finally think I've lost my mind.

When he'd found me, there was nowhere to go. I had nowhere else to hide. I had no choice but to get into his car. Now that I knew what he was capable of, I didn't want him to think that he needed to murder me too.

When I got into the car, I found my phone in the cupholder and assumed that Nash had grabbed it from my kidnapper. I put it in my pocket and braced myself because he pulled away before I had a chance to put on my seat belt. While it would have been automatic for me to put it on whenever I entered a vehicle, I was temporarily frozen in place. It was only when my phone vibrated in my pocket that I came out of it. I thought it had more to do with the shrilling ring coming from Nash's car. It could be a coincidence, but what was the likelihood that we'd both get text messages at the same time?

What I hadn't counted on was that Nash's text would appear on his dashboard and distract him. I skimmed the message and gasped.

You might have won this battle, but the war is far from over.

Nash mumbled under his breath and not once did he look over at me.

"What?"

"How could you?"

That forced me to look at him. "I have no idea what you're talking about."

"How could you betray me?"

The hurt in his voice couldn't be faked. "What? By leaving the way I did? I'm sorry, but I needed to get out of town for my safety."

"No, by trying to fuck my father."

There was nothing that could have prepared me for this moment. Was this what he'd thought for all of these years? Had murdering someone been the catalyst for finally telling me?

"Are you out of your mind? I would never in a million years... do you really think that little of me?"

I regretted the words before they left my mouth and wished I could take it back. Of course, he thought that this would be true. He hated me.

"Nothing seems to be out of the realm of possibilities with you, Goodwin."

"And you had no problem fucking someone you suspected slept with your father?"

"What's good for one Henson—"

"If you finish that sentence, I'm not going to be liable for my actions and there is a good chance that we'll get into a car accident tonight."

Anger clouded my judgment, and I really did want to hit him. I took several deep breaths before I continued. "Even though you don't fucking deserve anything from me, I swear on everything that I own, on everything that I love that I didn't do it. While I regret leaving how I did, it had nothing to do with trying to have sex with your father."

Nash didn't reply right away, and I assumed he was thinking about what I said.

I turned my attention back to the scene unfolding in front of me. We were driving up to a green light, and I prayed that the light would turn red. It might give me the chance that I needed.

My breath caught in my throat as I watched the light turn to yellow when we were several feet away, and Nash slowed the car down as if he was going to break.

"Then why did you leave, Raven?"

It had been the first time he said my first name since I'd arrived back in Brentson. Hearing him say my name hit me in a way that I hadn't been expecting. It almost robbed me of my breath, I hadn't realized how much I'd been waiting for him to say it. A part of me wanted to answer his question, but I saw that a potential opportunity was coming toward me, and I knew I had to take it.

Given the time of night and the lack of traffic, I knew the likelihood that this light would change back to green quickly was high. It was now or never.

It all happened so fast that I didn't think. I just acted, and I was sure that was driven by anger and despair.

As the car slowed down again, I pressed the unlock button and threw open the car door before diving out of the vehicle.

"Raven!"

The sound of him yelling my name would haunt me forever. It was a mixture of disbelief and anger. Fear might have been sprinkled in, or maybe I was just hearing what I wanted to.

I wasted no time getting up and running because I needed every second of a head start that I had on him. The mental shock from tossing my body out of a moving car plus the impact of my body hitting the ground should have derailed me, but my adrenaline kicked into high gear, and I just kept running. Where I was going, I didn't know, but anywhere seemed better than where I was.

Nash was a wild card, but so was I. I know he hadn't expected me to flee a moving vehicle or else he would have done more to secure it. Underestimating me was his mistake, not mine.

As my foot hit the ground again, part of me wanted to give up, to stop moving because my body was exhausted. The run through the woods from the Chevalier Manor had done a number on me, but my drive to survive was determined to carry me through.

What I hadn't counted on was Nash's stride being longer than mine and his athletic ability. I was too afraid that if I turned around to see how far away he was from me, it would cause me to slow down or fall. But over my own breathing, I could hear him, and it seemed as if he was gaining on me.

The hairs on the back of my neck stood at attention. It was as if he was breathing down my neck without him physically doing so… until he was.

I saw his arm out of the corner of my eye just before it wrapped around my waist. He pulled me into his body and before I could scream, his hand covered my face.

"I didn't want to do this," I thought I heard Nash say, but the words sounded jumbled. *What was happening?*

I tried to voice my thoughts, but nothing came out. Instead, my eyelids felt heavy, and all the fight left my body. I could feel myself collapsing, but there was nothing I could do to stop it.

The only choice I had was to embrace the darkness that fell over me.

And I did.

~

THANK YOU FOR READING! The next book in the series, Devious Secret, is available for pre-order now!

WANT to join the discussion about the The Brentson University Series? Click HERE to join my Reader Group on Facebook.

PLEASE JOIN my newsletter to find out the latest about the The Ruthless Billionaire Trilogy and my other books!

ABOUT THE AUTHOR

Bri loves a good romance, especially ones that involve a hot anti-hero. That is why she likes to turn the dial up a notch with her own writing. Her Broken Cross series is her debut dark romance series.

She spends most of her time hanging out with her family, plotting her next novel, or reading books by other romance authors.

briblackwood.com

ALSO BY BRI BLACKWOOD

Broken Cross Series

Sinners Empire (Prequel)

Savage Empire

Scarred Empire

Steel Empire

Shadow Empire

Secret Empire

Stolen Empire

The Broken Cross Series Box Set: Books 1-3

The Ruthless Billionaire Trilogy

The Billionaire's Auction

The Billionaire's Possession

The Billionaire's Vengeance

Brentson University Series

Devious Game

Devious Secret

Devious Heir

Merciless Reign Trilogy

Merciless Deception

Printed in Great Britain
by Amazon